Hope Under The Willow

a novel

Amanda J Kelley

Copyright © 2021 Amanda J Kelley

All rights reserved

The characters and events portrayed in this book are fictitious. Any similarity to real persons, living or dead, is coincidental and not intended by the author. The fictitious characters and locations are in no way accurate historical representations to mythological, religious, or cultural societies or systems; past or present. As a work of fiction this story is not historically accurate nor is it intended to be.

No part of this book may be reproduced, or stored in a retrieval system, or transmitted in any form or by any means, electronic, mechanical, photocopying, recording, or otherwise, without express written permission of the publisher.

ISBN: 9798580059129

Cover design by: KzoDesigns

Printed in the United States of America

Contents

Title Page
Copyright
Hope Under The Willow
One — 1
Two — 9
Three — 14
Four — 22
Five — 27
Six — 35
Seven — 43
Eight — 49
Nine — 61
Ten — 68
Eleven — 73
Twelve — 82
Thirteen — 88
Fourteen — 94
Fifteen — 101

Sixteen	106
Seventeen	111
Eighteen	118
Nineteen	126
Twenty	134
Twenty One	146
Twenty Two	150
Twenty Three	154
Twenty Four	162
Twenty Five	165
Twenty Six	171
Twenty Seven	176
Twenty Eight	181
Twenty Nine	188
Thirty	194
Thirty One	200
Thirty Two	205
Thirty Three	212
Thirty Four	218
Thirty Five	224
Thirty Six	229
Thirty Seven	234
End	237
Acknowledgement	239
About The Author	241
Books In This Series	243

Hope Under The Willow

a novel

Book One of Hope's Trilogy

One

Confused and alone, I was found on the side of the road. A kind man happened to see me as he was driving by. He pulled over and offered me a ride. That was when I realized there was a problem. I could not tell him where to take me. I could not even tell him my name. Too scared to stay and afraid to go with him, I curled in on myself and stayed silent. He did what he thought was right and turned me over to the authorities. That was fifteen years ago, but you would not be able to tell by the look of me. I still look like the same doe eyed teenage girl scared in the ditch.

At sixteen (the rough estimate of my age provided by doctors) the state tried to help me. Smart people dressed in smart clothes questioned me daily. Doctors examined me and took samples. I posed for pictures that were ran through local and national news presses. After two weeks, nothing came of any of it. Memories did not miraculously come back to me. No one called the hotlines to say they recognized me. I went through the process of getting a generic identification and placement in state care. Where they expected me to stay until I was no longer a minor. The name they gave me was plain, Jane. My unremarkable features, bland. The home I was assigned, was already too crowded. I doubt anyone noticed when I left. Leaving was the dumbest thing I could ever do. I walked out without food or clothes or money. I left the safety of four walls, and running water, to hide from drunks and police in the shadows of dumpsters. Things I did not think about when I took off. The decision was made though, and I was too proud to go back.

That's when I met Tracy. She found out I was living on the streets and sprang to action, introducing me to a woman who would take me in. Known as the *'Voodoo Queen'* to the locals. Though, I have never seen her practice any kind of Voodoo. She does however believe in metaphysics and aromatherapy. Her totems and dried herbs make people believe she works with potions and spells. When really, she makes the best teas I have ever tasted. I will never be able to thank her enough for taking me in. Felicia, with her thick southern accent, was barely less homeless than I was at the time. Living in a community of street people that had converted a single piece of abandoned property into a small urban village. She cleared a small room in her shack for me to sleep. Barely wide enough to stretch out completely. I found happiness in that simple place. I try not to think about the time before I met her.

Today, thanks to Tracy and Felicia, I am well enough off that I have a job and my own studio apartment. The small bathroom mirror reflects the auburn hair that falls in waves shaping my long face. Pale skin and blue eyes stare back at me. Leaning in, I look for creases near my eyes, streaks of silver around my temples. Nothing. Even on this day, my state appointed birthday, a total thirty-one years has not aged me far beyond my youth. It gets harder for my friends to ignore that I have not aged like they have. I have helped them to hide the time that has marked their skin and hair. Applying concoctions of stains and developers to hide the white streaks. Makeup to cover the fine lines that have appeared around their eyes. The teasing back and forth is getting harder to laugh off. A tension has started to form between us.

So, the apartment is trash, the rattling of the walls reminds me as someone walks down the hall outside my door. Three loud bangs against it echo through the studio. Running late as usual, I grab a bottle of pills out of the cabinet behind the mirror. As I dump the last pill in my hand, I make a mental note to ask Tracy to stop for a refill. I throw my purse over my shoulder and toss the pill in my mouth. Three more loud bangs against the door.

"I am coming." I call out. I rush before whoever is on the other side beats the door right out of the frame.

The door swings open too easily. Slamming against the counter to the kitchen side of the apartment. Tina shouts, "Happy birthday!" She wraps her arms behind my neck and twirls us around. The floorboards under our feet sigh in protest.

"We've been waiting outside for twenty minutes." Tracy scolds me. Her arms folded across her chest.

"I am ready now. Let's go." I push them both away from the door as I lock it behind me.

I even give the knob a little jerk. Pointless, I know. I could lean on it exactly right and knock it down. Not like I own anything worth stealing anyway. They are already headed down the stairwell by the time I turn back around. I jog to catch up to them. Tracy, and I, met Tina a handful of years ago. She is the promiscuous one of us. We do not mind it much. She always manages to get us free drinks with her charm.

Tracy over time, has fallen into the position of looking after us. Naturally, she can be very motherly. The cliché group of three friends. The responsible one, the wild child, and the one who is just along for the ride. Tracy makes sure that we always end up back at home or at the very least her house. Tina gives her the most reasons to need to be motherly. While it annoys Tina, I appreciate having someone look after us. Tracy seems to be perfectly happy with her role in our little trio.

We file out of the building to Tracy's car. I take the back seat. Tina jumps in the front passenger seat, checking her flawless makeup in the visor mirror before buckling her seatbelt. Tracy settles behind the wheel in the driver seat rolling her eyes at Tina. She winks in the rearview mirror at me as she tosses back a little orange bottle with a white lid.

"I thought you might be running low."

"You thought right." I say as I twist the top off.

Relief blows from my chest as I check inside to make sure the pills meet my standards. I started taking these things after I moved in with Felicia. I do not remember why. Now, I do not make it long without them. I would not know what it feels like to have a clear mind anymore. Before the pills I was a nervous wreck. How is a person supposed to function with no family, no home, and no memories of how she ended up here? Besides, Tracy would not let me get hurt. She understands why I need them. She *is* the one that introduced me to them.

Tina interrupts my internal thoughts, "We are going to be late and miss out on our table." She whines to Tracy.

Tracy rolls her eyes. "We will make it."

She puts the car in drive and peels out of the parking lot. The streetlights have started to come on. Neon lights click to life as we pass them by. Night is inching closer. I do not live far from the strip downtown. Tracy insists it is easier to get both of us home if she takes her car. "You try towing two drunks down main at three in the morning." She has said to us when we protest. Parking can be difficult to get close to our pub of choice. We usually end up having to walk a few blocks anyway. Tina starts chatting away. She is good at small talk. She does not seem to mind that I do not partake in the conversation. I sink into my seat as the first pill starts to blanket my mind in its peaceful cover.

Tracy pulls the car into an open spot on the same block as the pub. Tina is overzealous at the luck of finding a spot so close. I climb out of the car first. Adjusting my shirt, I notice two men watching us from across the street. Paranoia creeps up my neck. I grab one more pill from the bottle before tucking it away in my purse. Across the street, the men are gone when I look back again.

Tina pulls herself out of the car. Last, I might add. "Hurry up! I bet our spot is gone already." She loops her arm in mine and practically drags me down the sidewalk.

I look around once more looking for the men. Still not there. Dropping my arm away from Tina, I toss the pill in my mouth. The sidewalk ahead grows more crowded. People laughing, cars passing by us, music from inside the clubs we pass, and bright lights battle for my attention as the strip comes to life. Tracy and Tina have walked far enough ahead I feel like I am being left behind. I skip to catch up. They stop near the entrance.

Tracy is refusing something that Tina is offering her. "Why I keep company with you two blows my mind." Her face in a crooked grin.

Tina responds, but I do not catch her words over the ever-growing noise around me. I welcome the numbing sensation of the pills. Tonight, I am going to need them. I feel on edge already. I reach into my purse for my ID. I pull it out to hand to the door man. But Tracy and I are already sitting at a rickety two-top table. Our usual spot. Confused, I try to ask Tracy what just happened. She is staring dreamily across the room. A worn-out sofa sitting on the opposite wall. A couple is occupying the space. They cannot keep their hands off each other. I put the ID back in my purse. I reach my arm across the table to get Tracy's attention. Before I can ask her anything, she starts rambling about her most recent love affair. The sound of her voice floats away from my attention.

Searching the crowded room with my eyes, I ask, "Where is Tina?"

She ignores me or does not hear me. She continues talking. About a ...*truck driver*... *maybe*... I am not sure. I put my elbows on the table and rub my hands across my face. Resting my head there for a moment. Trying to pull myself together. I do not remember ever being this high before.

When I open my eyes again there is a drink in front of me. Something frozen and pink. On a napkin beside it, is one of my pills. Without considering it, I take the pill and a long swallow from the drink. I look back up at Tracy. *No, not Tracy, Tina. Has it been Tina the whole time?* She moves around the small table to pull me by my arm. A smile stretches her face.

   Giving in to her I stand. "Ok, ok. Let me get my purse."

   In the short span of turning to my purse and back, Tina is gone. I am sitting on a sofa, wrapped in a grey blanket. A pounding headache prevents me from investigating anything else. My eyes close against the pain. Tracy's voice registers to my ears. I flinch against the expected pain from the sound. The headache seems to be gone though. Barely opening my eyes, I glance down to the other end of the sofa, Tracy is chatting away. The blanket that I thought was around me is gone. This sofa is not the one at the pub. It is firm and clean. A strange pattern decorates the seat under me. It is like a waiting room bench more than a sofa. The back is low, and the armrest is square and hard.

   Realizing I am curled up and leaning heavily against the hard armrest, I reposition myself to straighten my spine. The room leans side to side as a wave of nausea rolls from my belly to the back of my throat. I close my eyes again and take a few deep breaths. When I open them, I slowly try to figure out where I am. Mentally marking the things that I see. Tracy is on the opposite end of the sofa. She is chatting away at someone across from her. Another sofa matching this one, faces ours. A man sitting, leaning forward, resting elbow to knees is listening intently to her. His fingers are knitted together as his thumbs fidget one over the other. I cannot make out his details. I cannot even tell what color his hair is. Everything is a blur. Anger flashes through me. I do not know why but the familiar heat of my frustration fills my shoulders. The room is filled with people. The women in cocktail dresses and men in suits. A blue sign catches my attention. A white stick figure wearing a dress. *A bathroom*, I push myself to stand. I let my mind find balance before I take the first step. The room around me leans at a sickening angle. *I am falling.*

I catch myself on a cold, solid surface. Upright, rather than flat on my face as I half expected. My fingers and palms flat against the hardness, my thumbs wrapping down a thin ledge. *A counter?* Directly in front of me the counter slopes gently down into a bowl with a metal circle in its center. Down the rest of the counter three more basins dip into the surface. *The bathroom?* I find myself in the mirror. My hair and makeup are done up like I spent an afternoon in Tina's beauty kit. I am wearing a deep blue cocktail dress. The bathroom is quiet. I must be alone. *I think I took too much. Can this night get any stranger? No, scratch that. Please do not let this night get any stranger.*

Two

My ears ache. A shrill laughter beating against them. I quail away from Tina, who is leaning into me. I think I missed the joke. She has changed into a dress too. She is heavily flirting with a man standing across from her. Maybe I am supposed to be her wingman. We do this often, to test out the 'feel' of someone. You know, just in case he is a weird-o. If this man is, we should have already run the other way. He is big and tall, with broad shoulders, and black hair. His suit is all black. And he is not alone. Another man standing just as big and tall as him, only with blond hair, is standing beside him. Tina does not seem to notice my discomfort or confusion. She chats away at them.

No longer in the bathroom, I look around to figure out where we are now. Three sides of the room look out onto other buildings. City lights twinkle around me. Stars dot the cloudless sky above us. It looks like we are floating above the city. Behind us a brick wall stands tall and plain. Only a single set of French doors interfering with the straight lines of the stones. We are not in a room at all. We are on a rooftop balcony. I have never considered myself acrophobic. I also have never been this high up. My stomach rolls again.

I turn back to Tina. She is gone. *Again.* The man with the black hair is still here, but Tina, and the blond-haired man, is gone. This man smiles at me and raises his glass in my direction. I return his smile with a polite one of my own and then head back toward the door. As my feet cross the threshold, I feel a wave of relief. I walked from one end of the balcony to here and I did not lose time or fall. Even if it is only a few yards of space and a few moments of time. I did it.

The relief does not last long. A deep voice calls out my name, "Janie." Not my name. The nickname that Tina calls me when she is purposely trying to annoy me. It works.

"It is Jane." I snap as I look for the source.

"Ah, but I prefer Janie." He teases.

Another man dressed in all black, approaches me from the other side of the room. A glamorous penthouse living room. *I do not belong here.* The man closes the distance between us. He is cocky and maybe even cute. The heat of my anger fills my shoulders again. I do not know him. I do not know where I am. I am not in any mood to play cat and mouse with this guy. He is as big as the other men and the look on his face is almost menacing. His hair is a chestnut brown with natural warm highlights from sun exposure. His eyes are light. Nearly a yellow shade of green in this low-lit room. I spot the exit behind him. He catches me by the arm as I try to ignore him and pass without acknowledging him. Not painfully, but tighter than I care for it to be.

My eyebrows pull together and down. I feel my nose lift in a sneer. "Let go of me." I hiss.

"Janie, don't be like that." He coos. "We were having such a good time." He tries to pull me closer to him.

I snatch my arm from his hold and spin away. Only to smack into someone else. *Tracy.* She teeters as she regains her balance. "Jane. Where are you going in such a rush?" She asks breathless from bumping into me. She puts her hands on my elbows to steady me.

She has changed too but I do not take the time to admire her. "I have to get out of here." I say in a rush. A panic adds to my tone that I was not aware I was feeling.

"Here, I have what you need." She fumbles through a small clutch she has tucked under her arm. She pulls out a bottle of pills and starts to open the lid.

I cover both of my hands over the bottle and push them back to her. "I think I have taken too much. I want to go home." Hysteria edging in my tone now.

"What you need is to calm down. Take one. I will get Tina. Then we can go."

She puts a pill in my hand and guides me to sit in an oversized chair. She disappears through the door leading to the balcony. I stare at the little pill in my hand. *Look at the trouble you caused.* I think to it.

"Changed your mind, huh?" His voice makes me jump.

My anger pulses up my neck. *Why is he back? Why am I still here?* I rest my head in one hand and put the pill in my mouth with the other one. Maybe it can make this man go away.

A hot, sticky, air moves close to my ear. "She isn't coming back for you." He whispers. I flinch away.

I shove him farther away from me and stand violently from the chair. Stomping across the room to the balcony. *Find Tracy and Tina and drag them away from here by their hair if I have to. Anything to get home.* I tell myself. The balcony is empty. Chairs sit vacant across the space. Tables stand alone with empty glasses and discarded napkins left by patrons. A scream builds in my throat and echoes into the night sky. I snatch a glass from the table closest to me and hurl it in the general direction of where I thought Tracy would be. The glass silently goes away. No sounds of it hitting the floor. No shattering glass. Just gone. *Oh no. Did I clear the side of the building? Is that glass plummeting to the city sidewalk below? What if it hits someone? Tomorrow's headline will read: 'Death by champagne glass, suspect unknown.'*

"Janie, the party has moved downstairs." The man says to me gently. "Come on. I will take you. I promise I won't bite; unless you ask me to." He teases.

I roll my eyes. Defeated, I allow him to take me to them. He guides me to an elevator as the pill starts to work. Time seeming to stretch forever in the small confines of the cube. Down and down. The elevator stops with a stifled *'ding.'* The doors slide open. My senses are brutally attacked by flashing lights, music so loud you can feel it in your chest, and a deep fog being sprayed across the floor by a machine. The man places a comforting hand on the small of my back and guides me away from the club-like area.

In the far back, Tracy and Tina are there with the other men from before. The man leading me does not take me to join them. The pill has definitely started to work. My emotions seem to have left themselves in the elevator. Together we sink into a dark corner with a perfect view of the dance floor, the spinning lights hardly reaching the shadows here. His comforting hand on my lower back snakes its way up my spine. Leaving a trail of chill bumps on my skin. He gently guides me to face him. Pulling my body close to his.

"Now, where were we?" He presses his lips to mine.

My mind reacts too slow to stop him. At first, I want to push him away, but my body defies me as I relax into his kiss. The vastness of him consumes me. An urgency speeds up my heart. Kissing him is unlike anything I have ever experienced. I latch my arms around his neck and squeeze our bodies closer together. A feeling I have never felt before. Something almost primal. If he lets go of me, I do not think I could stop myself from digging my nails into his flesh, sinking my teeth into his lip, and wrapping my legs around him to pin him to me. Because of the drugs, or the fear and confusion, I am not sure if I want to keep kissing him or hurt him.

Three

Thrashing and rolling, I fall out of bed. Not my bed. A bed covered in smooth, pink, satin sheets. In a room with sheer curtains and white walls. Not my apartment. I wait a moment to allow my heart to find an even rhythm. I shake away the lingering fog of sleep. Small memories of last night return as my brain calms. I hope most of them are just from a dream and not my reality. I steady myself as I stand and examine the room around me. Not Tracy's house either. Quietly I make my way out of the room and down a narrow hall. I pass two closed doors. One on either side. I consider peeking in. Then decide not to wake whoever may be inside. The end opens into a great room. Living room, dining room, and kitchen are separated only by the proper furniture grouped together.

This could be green-eyed guy's house. *My goodness, I do not even know his name.* I am still wearing the dress from last night. In the living room space, I search for my shoes and purse. Instead, I find a shopping bag with a brand-new pair of canvas shoes, a pair of shorts, and a t-shirt. Standing in the middle of the living room furniture I strip out of the dress and quietly put on the new stuff. *I am a thief now. This is now my life.* I scold myself. *What will Tracy think? I will give it all back.* I lie to myself.

I have never been on this end of a walk of shame.

I would really like no one else to see it. Out the front door, I quietly sneak. I am on a side of town that I do not recognize. My apartment, or even Tracy's house, is miles away. A car sits in the driveway. *No.* I tell myself as I open the door again. *Stop it.* I warn myself as I grab the keys conveniently hanging on a hook just inside. *I will return it later.* I refuse to acknowledge that stealing a car has far worse consequences than the outfit. I hop in the car and back out of the driveway before I can talk sense into myself.

I should have just walked. I am a paranoid mess the whole drive. It is hard to focus on the road ahead of me while I am trying to also watch all other corners around me. *The cops are going to find me. The drugs are still in my system. I am going to jail.* It takes me thirty minutes to get to Tracy's street. There is no way I could have walked that whole way. I park the car on the side of the road at the other end of the block. I leave the keys in the ignition. *Maybe someone else will grab it and this dilemma will disappear.* I do not even know myself anymore. I have never stolen anything, I have never woken up in a stranger's house, and I have never had such a bad reaction to the drugs. *Pills. Not drugs. Drugs are bad for you. I need the pills. They help me. It is official I have hit rock bottom. I need help.*

I jog down the street the rest of the way to Tracy's house. I skip up the steps and walk in through the front door. She has never locked her doors when she is home, and I am grateful to be behind the protection of these familiar walls. The strong smell of coffee is coming from the kitchen.

"Hey! What happened to you? We were wondering where you disappeared off to." Tina says, pouring a cup of coffee.

Already making my way to Tracy's bedroom, I talk back at Tina. "I was hoping you two might be able to help me fill some gaps. Is Tracy still in bed?"

Tina tries to warn me. "Yes, but..." It is too late. I have already swung the door to Tracy's room open.

With a cheery tone I belt, "Tracy, get up."

She yawns. "I'm up. I'm up." Groggily sitting up. "I knew you would turn up. There is some left over in the spare bathroom."

She waves me away. The door to her on-suite bathroom opens. The man with black hair from last night comes out wrapped in a towel. Feeling awkward, I head for the guest bathroom. The first thing Tracy said to me was about the pills. Like that would be the only reason I came here. *Is it the only reason I came here?*

Reaching for the handle of the bathroom door, it turns before I touch it. I jump back and a small *'yelp'* escapes my lips. The door swings inward revealing another shirtless man. The blond-haired guy from the party. His face changes as he looks at me. "Hi." He says curtly as he passes by me to join Tina in the kitchen.

I dive into the bathroom and slam the door closed. I lean against the sink and glance at myself in the mirror. No wonder he looked at me so strangely. My hair is bent at awkward angles and the makeup that was once on my eyelids now shadows the underneath of my eyes. I dig through the drawers under the vanity for a washcloth and hairbrush. I find the pill bottle Tracy mentioned. I ignore it and complete my first mission. After washing my face and taming my hair, I tidy the mess I have made. The bottle of pills looks at me again. I check myself in the mirror again. Better, not great, but an improvement.

The bottle of pills looks at me again. This time I pick it up. *I do not need them.* I tell myself. I open the bottle. Four little pills sit in the bottom of the orange container. Scolding myself in the mirror, I dump one into my hand. I put the cap back on and shove the bottle in my back pocket. I twiddle the pill in between my fingers. *Today could be the day.* I could keep moving forward and not look back. I could tell myself not to take it. Last night was not how it normally is. I never want to feel that way again. I do not even remember most of the night at all. *I could do it. I could put them down and walk away. Never look back.* I am lying to myself.

The pill bottle bulging in my back pocket and a single pill in my hands, I go back to the kitchen with the others. The four of them are sitting around the table with their coffee cups. The chatter stops. The awkward silence is interrupted by an insistent dinging sound. Tina hops out of her chair happily. She stops the alarm on the timer and begins to pull something out of the oven. I have never seen her cook. It smells delicious. She clatters away with her work.

Tracy clears her throat. "This is Luke." She gestures towards the man closest to her. The one with black hair. "This is Liam." She gestures across the table to the blond-haired man. She leans into Luke.

Tina brings two plates to the table. Setting them in front of the men. Some sort of pastry centers each plate. She would have had to start these incredibly early this morning if she made them from scratch. It is more likely that they are reheated after she bought them from the bakery. She makes a second trip with two more plates. No one speaks. No one looks at me. Then it hits me. They were not expecting me. I am interfering on whatever this is they are doing.

I take a step towards the door. "I think I am going to go home." I turn away from them.

Slowly walking away, waiting for a protest. One does not come. Over the last twenty-four hours our entire dynamic seems to have shifted. I reach the front door before I finally hear voices. They are chatting amongst each other. It stings. This feeling of rejection. Heat from my anger replaces the sting. I consider yelling at them. Stomping back in there and demanding an explanation. I twist the pill in my fingertips as I jerk the door open hard and slam it behind me. On the front porch I pause to slow my heart. The anger grows in my shoulders. *If I can calm myself down this time, without the pill, that will be a good first step.* I think it. I really do. But my hand brings the pill to my lips. I swallow. I scold myself, *well that did not last five minutes.* I shake off the disappointment in myself and walk off the porch. The closer I can make it to my apartment before the pill starts to work, the better chance I have to make it to my apartment at all. I do not make it far from Tracy's front porch before I hear someone calling my name. *Maybe they have had a change of heart and realize how upset I am.*

Only the voice is not coming from the direction of the house behind me. It is in front of me. "Jane." The man with the green eyes is making his way up the driveway.

I panic. "I am really sorry about the car. I parked it down there."

"I am not worried about the car." He does not even look back to where I pointed. "Jane, are you, all right?"

Moving in a wide arch to put distance between us, I try to skip passed him. At least he is not calling me that awful nickname anymore. *Why would he care if I were all right? How did he know I would come here?* He starts to move in my direction, closing the space I have put between us. The panic increases, adrenalin along with it. "I am fine. Sorry, I have to go." I pick up my pace.

He rushes to get in front of me, stopping me from moving forward by putting both of his hands against my shoulders. "Jane, did you take more? Did she give you more?" His eyes search my eyes for answers to his questions. *His blue eyes. Not green.* "Now we have to begin again." He sounds defeated.

I could have sworn his eyes were green. My mind is too preoccupied to think about what he is saying. I try to remember back. The lighting in the room could have made them look different. The pills could have also altered how I remember things. He also is not using the nickname he claimed to prefer. He squeezes my shoulders gently to get my attention.

"I really need to get home. I have to work tonight."

His hands move down my arms to my wrists. His grip gets tighter. "Do you have more on you now?" He asks.

I pull against his hold. "Let me go." The pill has not started to work yet. The adrenalin in my system kicks up and I shake with fear.

"Where is it?" He grits his teeth.

He holds one wrist tighter and drops the other. Before I have a chance to take advantage of my free arm, he spins me around. Somehow getting both of my arms pinned under one of his. My back against his chest. He starts patting against my pockets. He quickly finds the bottle.

"Get off of me!" I stomp my feet and arch my back. Trying anything to loosen his grip on me.

"I am sorry I have to do this." He says into my ear. "I won't leave you again. We have to start over. Do you understand?" He asks. "Please Jane." He begs. "I am trying to help you. I will help you."

My nose lifts in a sneer. The heat of my anger grows up my spine. *I do not know this man. I sure as hell do not need his help.* He feels the shift in my emotions. I draw in a deep breath to let out the loudest scream I can manage. Ready, his hand comes down hard across my mouth. Smothering the sound. I struggle against him. I try to bite his hand. I push against him with my body. I try to stomp his feet. Nothing I do works.

"I need you to stay calm." He begs me again. "I am going to help you, I promise."

The buzz reaches my brain then. The pill starting to work faster with the help of my beating heart. I hear more voices. I look around. We have moved from the driveway. *I was making progress. I should not have given up.* None of that matters now. My mind is getting fuzzy. The voices around me get louder. I cannot make out the exact words. My eyes finally find Tracy. She is standing on her porch. The black-haired man, Luke is standing with her. They are not looking at me. They face each other. Luke seems to be angry. Tracy's head drops and she walks back inside her house.

She left me. She is allowing this to happen to me. I took another pill making myself incapable of fighting against this and she is not doing anything. She walked away from me, leaving me trapped in a stranger's hold. How stupid am I that I could not wait just moments more before I took that pill? How stupid am I to think that my best friend would stand up for me? My vision blurs. Not because of the pills. Because of the tears that fill them.

I feel it as it happens this time. The pill works its way through my system. This time I know that the drug is going to take me to a different time and place. These events will blur into my damaged memory. This time I submit to it. I let it erase the betrayal I feel. I let it wash away the fear. At least this time, I knew it was going to happen. It is my own fault.

Four

I wake in the room with the pink sheets again. I do not bother sitting up. I let my eyes gently open. My brain foggy. I remember being here before. I remember taking clothes that were not mine and stealing a car. If I just go back to sleep maybe I can pretend it was all just a dream. A soft tap on the door lets me know that that is not in the cards for now.

"Hi." He says quietly. "I am sorry I wasn't here when you woke up before. It was dumb of me to leave you alone. I knew you would wake up scared and confused." He pauses, waiting for a reaction from me. "I am sorry." He says again.

I adjust myself to sit up and look at him. He watches me cautiously. Waiting for me to do something rash. I can tell by his ready stance, by the dart of his eyes at every move I make, and the bottom lip that he is currently gnawing at.

"Who are you?" I cannot decide if he is the same man from before. His eyes are blue again today.

He relaxes slightly and takes one step forward. I flinch away from him. He stops and clears his throat, "My name is Lane." He rubs his hands together and looks around the room. "I don't want to overload you with information. It is an exceptionally long story."

"I have time." To myself I think, I imagine I have already lost my job. My friends are probably not going to come for me. What else do I have to do?

His hands press together at his chest, as if he is praying. "In time, I will tell you everything I know. First, we need to get you off the drugs."

My eyebrows scrunch. "What is your interest in my sobriety?"

"It is important that you are healthy and able to make your own decisions." He puts one hand up as if to tell me to hold on. He disappears down the hall for only a blink of time. Returning with a tray. "Before you move, I have something to warn you of." He sets the tray on the end table and moves slowly and deliberately. He lifts the sheet from the foot of the bed revealing my outstretched legs.

"What the fuck is that?" Around my left ankle is a large metal cuff with a thick chain attached from it to somewhere under the bed.

"Many of your days here have been exceedingly difficult and this is the only solution I can come up with; aside from having you placed in a facility actually equipped for this kind of thing. I thought I understood detox was difficult. But I guess, you don't really know until you live it." His lips lift on one side in an attempt at a sympathetic smile.

"I didn't ask for help to get sober. It is just pills. It is not like it is the hard stuff. Last night was just a rough one. I just need to go home." He does not respond. I pull my knees to my chest, testing the weight of the cuff. I wrap my arms around my legs and rest my forehead on the top of my knees. What he said finally registers in my brain, "Days?"

I hear him take a deep breath. I refuse to look up. "This is the third time I have brought you here. The first time was just by chance. You were out of it. You slept it off on the couch before taking off. This past weekend your friends were making some bad decisions. We do not typically step in like we did with you. We are supposed to just observe. Your friends kept feeding you pills. I was concerned that you were going to overdose and no one around was stepping in to help you." He pauses. "Three days is how long it took you to come down. When you were gone this morning, I panicked. I am sorry for treating you like I did when I found you."

"How many days between all of this?" Tears fill my eyes. I tuck my head farther in my knees.

"Well, I guess the first night you slept off was technically Friday morning a week ago. Then," he pauses to think, "it was early Sunday morning that I brought you here hoping you would stay. That was the start of the worst three days."

"Today is…"

"Wednesday." He finishes my sentence.

There is a long moment of silence. I am afraid that if I open my mouth to speak sobs will flow out of it uncontrollably. I have never lost almost two weeks of time. Well, not since I was found. I do not feel angry or scared,

I feel confused and something else that is not quite reaching my brain.

I internally kick myself for taking that pill on Tracy's porch. Maybe if I had not taken that one, maybe if I would have waited just a few more seconds, I would not have taken it at all. I could handle what is going through my brain right now. I could maybe even understand what I need to do next. But, for now, all I want to do is cry.

He breaks the silence, "I think that is enough for now. I am going to leave you here. I will just be in the living room if you need anything at all. You can reach the bathroom over there and I will leave the food here. Take your time, there is no hurry, but I would suggest a shower soon. I, uh, do not know how long it has been since your last one and… I think it may help you feel better."

Wow, he just told me I stink. He is probably right. I do not hear him leave. When I lift my head, he is gone. I look first at the food. A simple sandwich, bag of chips, an orange, and a plastic cup of water. I gingerly move my legs to hang off the side of the bed. The chain follows raining down in a heap on the floor. I bounce the leg that it is attached to. The weight is noticeable, but it is not very heavy. I take the water and orange with me as I move to the bathroom. The chain jingles behind me with every step. Chink, chink, chink.

If I stay here and let him help me get clean, then I could possibly go back to my normal life. Or I could even start a whole new life. I could do even better this time. All these years wasted. I could go back to school. Get a real job. It is nice to dream about living in a home like this one. With solid walls and separate rooms. I imagine for a moment that this could be my own room. A room with its own private bathroom and a closet with actual doors instead of crudely hung curtains. It is a nice dream. I should have thought about that before I ran away from that girl's home. I have been on this path too long to get to go back now. My goals need to be smaller. More achievable.

Step one: Get a shower. The bathroom is average sized. A shower tub combo, a toilet, and a single sink vanity. Above the toilet there are a couple of shelves with towels, wash cloths, and a small stack of folded clothes. I consider how I am supposed to get dressed and undressed until I notice I am only wearing a long t-shirt dress. I try not to overthink how or who changed my clothes for me. I choose to believe that at some point I made that decision. The stack of clothes is more of the same long t-shirt dresses.

Have I already decided to stay?

Five

A day passes. The drug leaves my system. Sickness and pain replace it. Withdrawal sets in. Headaches, nausea, and paranoia consume the world inside this bedroom. It started slowly. I thought I could handle it. Now I am not so sure. I want to cut my leg off and escape. I would do anything for one more pill. Just to make this all stop. I have tried to reason with him. If I ween myself off them it will not be this hard. He does not argue with me. He does not say anything during my fits. I have thrown the trays of food he has left for me. I have made and unmade the bed a half dozen times. In calm moments I have tried to shower. Tried to refresh myself. Standing for that long makes me dizzy causing the headache and nausea to hit harder. Followed shortly by another fit of anger. He stays away for the most part. Only entering the room during times that I am calm. It does not stop me from throwing my words at him.

During the short minutes of calm, like now, I feel guilty. He is only trying to help me. I have said some awful things to him. He keeps coming back. He keeps on cleaning up the messes I make. He does not react to my words. Once I think I even hit him with the chain. He was only trying to stop me from hurting myself. I snatched away with the chain in my hand. The slack of it whipped him across the arm. I regret it, but I did not apologize. He did not act like it hurt that bad anyway. Though, now I am sure it did.

Days pass like this. I do not know how many. Every minute that I am awake feels like an eternity. When I am asleep, nightmares haunt me. The calm moments that I find are filled with the broken memories over the last couple of weeks. Revelations that I do not want to face.

Tracy is the one that started giving me the pills. All the way back to the alley. It could have been the very day she discovered I was living on the street. She has continued to be the one to keep me in full supply. As far as I know, everyone around me knew about them too. Felicia had to have known. Her shack is too small to keep secrets. Not to mention her keen since of intuition. Did she approve of my taking them? I even think Tina has taken them with me on a few occasions. That could just be my mind attempting to give reason to why I have always taken them, in a '*she did it too*' way of excuse.

None of this changes that the pills that I was taking most recently definitely affected my body differently than any I have ever taken before. They did not look different. I do not even know what they, or any of the others, are made for. I cannot tell you if they are a legal substance that I illegally obtained and abused. Or, if they are manufactured by street thugs preying on the vulnerable to make a dollar. I do know that I never want to feel that way again. I do not know if I am strong enough not to.

Sitting on the bed staring out the window, lost in self-reflection, a loud banging echoes down the hall coming from the front door. I quietly slide off the bed eager for any kind of distraction from my own mind.

I hear the door creak open and then a man's voice, "Liam told me what you are doing."

Lane responds to the angry voice with calmness. "Luke, I have it under control." The way he talks to me when I am on a rage. I peer around the door frame.

"He knows too. He won't be happy about this." Luke warns. I wonder who this '*he*' could be.

I must have made a noise. Luke snaps his head to look at me. "What the fuck Lane? You have it chained in there." The look on his face scares me and I duck back into the room.

Lane's voice stays calm, "Just go. This has nothing to do with his plan. This is my own thing."

I press myself against the wall inside the bedroom hoping to hide from the rage that seems to fill the entire house. I can almost feel it growing from Luke.

"Everything we do is his plan. We cannot get distracted, Lane." Luke is nearly shouting. "He will come. He will end it."

I think I hear Luke pacing. I risk a peek around the door frame. His fists are balled up and he is breathing deeply. He paces in wide steps, like a lion on the prowl.

"The less you are involved the better it will be for you." Lane tells him. I do not understand how he can stay calm with the wild animal pacing in front of him.

"I won't defend you, neither will Liam. You have done this to yourself brother."

Oh, brother. They are family. Why do I feel guilty?

Lane does not respond. He crosses his arms over his chest. His body saying that he is done with the conversation. The rage emanates around Luke. It moves the air around him. *I must still have drugs in my system.* I tell myself. Luke stops toe to toe with Lane. His broadness doubles Lane's. The veins in his neck pulse. I barely have time to register what is happening when he lets a fist go flying through the space between them, landing at the Lane's jawline.

His head snaps back and he drops his arms. He does not move to defend himself or to deliver his own punch. An emotion passes his face. He does not act on whatever it is. He just stands there eyeing Luke. Luke takes one step back, turns his head to give me the most threatening look I have ever seen. He lets out a huff while turning on his heel and slamming the door behind him.

Lane stands there for a long time, unmoving. When he finally relaxes, I let out a breath I did not know I was holding. His attention returns to me. A bruise has already started to form on his lower cheek.

"He is right." I do not know why I am taking Luke's side. "I could find help on my own. I am not your responsibility. You should be with your family."

He shakes his head and massages the bridge of his nose with two fingers. "They will come around." He pauses. More to himself than me, he says, "This was part of his plan. Luke doesn't understand that it is better this way."

"He just punched you in the face." I remind him.

"That seems a little worse than not understanding something."

"Luke has the worst temper of all of us." He pauses. "Things are changing. The way he had it planned seemed wrong. He is rushing it. There was supposed to be more time. I do not think he is right anymore. Luke and Liam will figure it out." He looks back at me. Judging my reaction.

I think about my next question carefully. There are so many of them spinning through my brain. Who is this 'he'? What is the plan for? "What do I have to do with all of it?" Is the question that my selfish mind asks.

"We will find out together." He answers as he makes his way down the hall and turns into one of the rooms I have not been in yet. I hear him shuffling through cabinets. A sink turns on. More shuffling. "Would you mind some company for lunch?" He asks as he walks out of what I now believe is a bathroom and makes his way toward the kitchen area.

"Are we going to talk about this?" I ask. He does not answer me. Feeling my own frustration building I take a deep breath. I move to the center of the room to sit in the floor. It is not long before he comes in with a tray full of sandwiches, drinks, and chips, enough for two. He sits across from me on the floor placing the tray between us. "I thought for sure a bruise was forming on your face from that punch." I say to him as he picks up the first sandwich.

He responds curtly, "I don't bruise easily."

"Are you going to tell me what that was all about?"

I ask again.

He chews quietly. I pick up a sandwich. I take a small bite. I wait to see if the nausea returns. I do not realize he is watching me until he says, "I think it is too soon to talk about it." He waits for me to respond.

I consider what he is saying. I am a ticking time bomb waiting to explode. I cannot even eat without worry that my body will reject it. The information that he is holding could flip the switch on that bomb. I decide not to respond to him. He is right. I do not want to admit that aloud.

He gathers the tray and remnants of the lunch and carries them away. I wonder if I offended him in some way. He did not say anything else while we ate. He hardly looked at me at all. I move to sit on the bed and stare out the window. In the early morning, the sun's rays invade the bedroom with her bright light directly across my face. Now, the light is bright but somewhere else in the sky. Possibly afternoon time.

Restless, I pace the room. The clink, clink, clink of the chain attached to my ankle, the only sound in the house. I make the bed meticulously. There is only a single pillow in a case, a fitted sheet, a flat sheet, and a thicker blanket. I wipe down the few surfaces in the room with a cloth from the bathroom. I clean the bathroom.

He has not left me any cleaning chemicals, so it is more like wiping things down with a wet cloth. Then going back to dry it all with a dry cloth. The cabinets under the sink are mostly empty but I arrange the toothbrush, toothpaste, hairbrush, and floss in evenly spaced lines ordered by height. I position the shampoo, conditioner, and soap on a small shelf built into the wall of the shower tub combo. I pull the shower curtain evenly closed. I organize the clean linens on the shelves. I pace some more, fiddle with the chain, sit in the floor, lay across the bed, before finally sitting cross legged in the floor in front of the door that leads down the hall. I sit and wait.

I lose myself in thought. How long have I been here this time? Are Tracy and Tina looking for me? Does Felicia know I am missing? Am I a missing person? They must have an idea of where I am. They know who took me. I think Liam and Luke must both be his brothers, and they were at Tracy's the last time I seen them all.

The truth whispers in my brain. *They are not coming for me.* I shake that thought away. I cannot dwell on what part they play in all of this. Especially when I do not understand what all of this is. The memory of her turning away from me the last time I was at her house stings. A memory that I was hoping would wash away with the drugs. I turn my attention away to distract myself.

Through the window the sun has moved somewhere in the sky. It must be low in the sky. Twilight is slowly creeping to night. I hear a shuffle from the front of the house. Lane's broad shoulders fill the end of the hall. The lack of light in the hall paired with the full lighting behind him makes him look like a shadow. "I am going to prepare dinner. You should shower while I get it together."

I consider what he has said. "I am not very hungry right now. Do I have time to take a bath instead?" I hate myself for asking permission. Then scold myself for being ungrateful that he is feeding me and keeping me safe without me giving anything back for it. He nods.

Six

I fill the tub and ease down into the warm water. With the faucet at my feet and my back towards the door I lean against the wall of the tub basin. My head rests against the shower wall. The lip of the tub basin supports my neck. I have never had a tub to bathe in. People always talk about relaxing baths and spending hours in a tub of hot water, now I understand the allure. The heat of the water releases tensions in the muscles of my body that I did not realize were there.

Since lunch I have made it without the intense side effects of my withdrawal. I know I am not magically healed. I know that, given the chance, I would try to find a pill to take. I do not know much about addiction, but I am sure that is something I will struggle with for a long time.

The skin on my fingers starts to wrinkle. I consider getting out when Lane announces, "Dinner will be ready in about twenty minutes." His voice is close.

I look back over my shoulder to see him standing near the door. His back is to me. Facing away from the bathroom. From this view I can make out his profile. Smooth skin wraps over the hard lines of his bone structure. The hard line of his nose slopes down before rounding back sharply to the curve of his top lip. His bottom lip pouts above the square line of his chin and jawline. I snap my head away from him. Emotions stir inside me. The memory of that kiss. I shake the thoughts away.

"I won't be long." I respond feeling embarrassed.

"Let me know when you are decent." He tells me. I hear the soft thumps of his steps as he leaves the bedroom down the hall. The sound fades until I no longer hear them.

I sit a few minutes more. The attraction to him from before cannot be trusted. My mind was clouded with the chemicals I was putting in my body. Although my mind may be clearing now, I still cannot trust this feeling. I should not be feeling this at all. He is holding me captive in his house. Stockholm syndrome. It is merely a response to my isolation and my body trying to fill the void of the pill. I am eager for the connection and dynamic of easy conversation and human interaction. Tina, or Tracy, was always around. When they were not, I was at work. This is a normal response, to desire companionship. It is more important that I get healthy. Connect with myself before building relationships with anyone else.

I shake the lonely feelings away. My job has most likely replaced me by now. My apartment has probably evicted me already. The landlord is quick to put you out if he does not receive payment. My belongings are probably scattered on the sidewalk. Being picked through by street scavengers.

I carefully stand in the tub. The bottom is slick under my feet. A sudden slam from the front of the house stops me in my tracks. I stand frozen, waiting, willing myself to listen. Two voices vibrate through the wall. Lane's and someone I do not recognize. The voices grow louder and harsher. An argument. Maybe Luke has come back. Something sounds like glass as it crashes to the floor. A rumbling sound moves down the hallway. The mirror on the wall rattles. A stampede crashes into the bedroom. I wrap my arms around myself and push my body against the wall of the shower. I try to make myself small and hide from whatever threat has just showed up. I hear the familiar sound of fists hitting flesh. A couple grunts of pain and growls of exertion.

I stare through the door into the bedroom. I cannot see anything yet, but I know that whatever is happening is making its way in here.

"Don't!" Lane demands. The harshness of his word makes me jump.

A man's figure fills the doorway. I sink back farther, with nowhere to go. He is large and broad like Luke. His shoulders, so wide, I do not know how he will make it through the frame of the door. His hair is pure white. The strong features of his face draped with the wrinkles of time and age. He looks me up and down once before spotting the chain that is still around my ankle leading past him and to the bed. I watch the thought cross his mind before he leans down and picks up the chain. He holds the weight of it in his hand and a menacing sneer pulls his face into a threating sort of smile.

Lane growls, "Don't do it." I can hear his breath filling his chest and huffing out. "Leave, now!" He demands.

"I'll be on my way soon." The man says in a low growl of his own. His teeth grit and I see the chain pull taught before I can react to what is about to happen.

My head slams against the wall as my foot is pulled from under me. Stars dance in my eyes as water fills all my senses. I am under for only a second before I find a grip on the side of the tub to pull my head up and take a breath. My chest heaves in coughs trying to expel the water that made its way into them in the short second under. A large hand fills my view and shoves down hard. Underwater again, I claw at the arm holding me down. My legs thrash trying to contact anything that may help free me. Just as suddenly as the hand was there it is gone, and I am sitting up choking out the water in my lungs.

After a moment of confusion, I see the two men in a wrestling match in the small space of the bathroom. I snatch the drain plug to release the water and jump out. I skirt around the bodies struggling in the floor. I almost make it to the frame of the bed before my foot is snatched from under me again. My chest slams into the floor knocking what little breath I had back out. A wheezing sound fills my ears as my body tries to breath. I will myself to move. The chain pulls me backward a few inches. A weight crushes down on my back. My lungs lose the battle of trying to expand as they are forced to contract under the weight.

The end of the chain that is attached to the bed, lifts into the air violently. I flinch expecting it to hit me in the face. Instead, it wraps around my neck. The weight on my back lifts, and my lungs inflate pulling in as much air as they can hold. The chain tightens and the air is now trapped in my lungs causing a new kind of pain. The chain pulls tighter. A shadow fills my vision. My face feels like it may explode. The pounding of my heartbeat behind my ears grows louder and then stops.

Darkness and silence. Fear and pain. My face is pressed in the carpet. Breath escapes my lips and pulls back in painfully. A cough rocks my chest and pain shoots through my entire body. The pounding behind my ears resumes. My legs find their way under myself. My arms push into the floor below me.

I think I have myself in a strong enough position to move, a painful force slams into my ribs. The force knocks me from the foot of the bed to the wall under the window. My mind screams at me to get up. My body stays limp. Pain burning and pulsing everywhere. In my mind, a yelling grows louder. The yelling is not coming from my mind. Seconds pass before it registers that the yelling is Lane.

"Get up! Take the cuff off!"

My eyes adjust. The scene in front of me is Lane on the floor holding back the other man in a twist of arms and legs. The man's face is red with rage. He elbows Lane in the side. I jump as I fear he will get free and come after me again. I sit up too quickly for my brain. The room swirls in front of me. I pull the ankle with the cuff towards me and begin trying to push it off.

"Pull the latch!" Lane yells between grunts of the push-and-pull happening between him and the man.

They are now both on their knees facing one another. Each trying to stand before the other. The man lands a hard punch across Lane's face. Blood spatters from his lip. I return to my task of getting the cuff off in a rush. A single latch sits on the inside. It flips up and the cuff falls away. Disbelief is followed by the heat of anger in my shoulders.

Another sound of fist contacting flesh pulls my attention back to the struggle. I grab the cuff end of the chain. I rush across the room. With all my strength I jump on the man's back and wrap the chain around his throat. He stands easily with me on his back. I pull on the chain to no avail. He overpowers me easily. Slamming my body into a wall. I lose grip and fall to the floor. I land in the hallway. He turns to me. Flipping around I run down the hall. Ignoring the sounds of slams against the walls behind me. I tiptoe around the broken glass in the kitchen floor, searching for anything that could be a weapon. A knife block sits in the back corner of the countertop. I grab the largest looking handle and I am pleased when a wide long blade glints in the overhead light.

Holding the knife at my side ready to strike, I wait for them to come into the open area. "You fight me over this thing?" The man bellows.

I plant my feet, pull the knife up higher, ready to strike as Lane responds, "She isn't hurting anyone. This has nothing to with you." His breathing is heavy.

"You are putting us all at risk keeping that thing here." The man growls.

"I won't let you kill her. If he comes, I will handle that too." His voice almost sounds pleading.

I am shocked by my own anger as the heat of it builds in my shoulders. This man just tried to kill us. How can he try to reason with him? He was not trying to kill us, I realize. Only me.

"How will you ever take a house seat if you can't make the tough decisions for the better of our kind?" The man asks.

"I am not taking a house seat. Luke is better suited for that position anyway."

I have no idea what they are talking about. I remind myself that no matter what relationship the two of these men share, this man just tried to kill me. If I let my guard down, he will finish the job.

The man lets out a single, "Ha!". Then explains, "Luke is a hot head. He will never be a leader. Besides, the position is yours. You do not get the choice." I hear his footsteps coming down the hall getting closer. "After I finish this, your head will clear, and we can get back on track. No more distractions."

He crosses the threshold from the hallway to inches from where I am standing. I strike. He catches my arm midair. He laughs.

"Leave her!" Lane shouts. He quickly closes the distance between him and the man.

With his free hand, the man swings and again contacts Lane's face. I flinch watching Lane's head snap back so hard this time he loses his footing and falls to the floor. I snarl and try with all my might to push the knife into this man's chest.

He laughs again. "Look at this." He looks at me strangely. He twists my arm until the pain is unbearable. I drop the knife to the floor. Faster than I can see how he does it. My arm is free, and his hand is around my throat. The pressure on the veins in my neck, as opposed to restricting my breathing. "I've changed my mind." The man says. "You have always been able to handle anything I have thrown at you. This though, may break you." He glares at Lane, who is now standing in the hall.

Cautiously waiting. His bruised face changes. Fear. I usually cannot tell what he is thinking. This time it is clear to read, he fears whatever threat this man just made. I do not understand the meaning behind it. His fear is infectious. It wraps me up.

"You understand what I am saying." The man states satisfied with himself.

The man does not have a single mark on him. His hair and clothes are disheveled but no marks or blood. I realize Lane never hit him back. He restrained him, pulled him away, and told him to stop. But he never once struck this man. This man that beat on him. This man that holds my life in his hands as these thoughts cross my mind.

Lane keeps his voice low and calm. "Don't do this."

"I will see you both, Friday." He tosses me backwards. My thigh lands on a few shards of the broken glass. I quickly push myself away from the glass. I do not see the man leave. The front door clicks closed. Silence pours over the room.

Seven

The silence left in the wake of the man, is broken by the opening, and closing of a door in the hallway. Lane appears, holding a towel in my direction. I reach for it with a flinch. His face changes as he notices the broken glass and blood. I take the towel to cover myself. Still naked from the bath and now bleeding in the kitchen floor. Lane makes quick work of cleaning up the glass from the floor. He pulls a box from one of the cabinets. Kneeling beside me, he begins to clean and assess my wounds. I flinch as he makes easy work of removing the glass and covering the small gashes. The amount of blood that has puddled beneath me is more than I expected these small incisions could produce. He cleans that up too.

He scoops me up. I flinch as the jostle reminds me of all the other pains in my body. He carries me back to the bedroom and sets me on the bed gently. He looks at me for a long moment before he starts to turn to leave.

"Are we not going to talk about what the hell just happened?" I ask.

He stops moving away but keeps his back to me. "Why didn't you run?" He asks me.

I ignore his question and ask my own, "I was never

really trapped here, was I?"

"No, you weren't." He answers. Then asks again, "Why didn't you run?"

"The marks on your face look really bad." I do not have an answer for his question.

I should have run as soon as I knew the chain was off. I should have noticed earlier that the cuff was not locked. The hours I spent fiddling with that thing. The many times it got in my way. When all along I could have just taken it off. Walked right out the front door. I know he would not have stopped me. He has not been rough with me since outside of Tracy's house. Which he apologized for profusely.

"I will be fine." His shoulders kind of slump down. "I'm going to clean up. I will be right back." He walks out of the room.

I limp off the bed and to the bathroom. I hear his muted movements through the wall. I hear the shower start through the echo of the pipes inside the wall. I look at myself in the mirror. My hair is still wet. My neck is mostly red, with spots of purple forming in a crooked line of dots from under my chin on one side then angling down toward my collar bone on the other side. I gently run my fingertips along the line.

In the mirror I see the purpling of a bruise starting just above my wrist on my forearm. I open the towel to examine my side. A very dark purple oval covers most of the side under my arm, across my ribs. I gently push against it, testing the pain. I flinch. I sigh and lean against the vanity. I run my hands through my hair. My palm rubs against a golf ball sized knot on the back of my head. I flinch at the contact and then flinch as the pain in my ribs dispute the movement. Naked and abused. Humiliated and bruised. Never have I been this bad off before. These past couple of weeks have started a list of firsts for me. Firsts that I never imagined I would ever be checking off.

I feel his presence before I see him hovering in the doorway. He is clean and all the marks on his face are gone. Except for the swollen side of his lips, you would not know he was just in a fist fight. He holds out a stack of clothes to me. I flinch again as I reach for them.

His face changes as he watches me. "I shouldn't have brought you here." I do not respond to him. I do not know what to say. "I thought I could protect you. Stop him. I was wrong."

"Why?" Is the only word that comes out of my mouth. My throat is sore, and the sound of my voice is raspy and deep.

I hear his breath catch. I do not look up to meet whatever emotion may be on his face. I feel weak and stupid. He decides to answer this question. "My family is... different. In our world things are... different. There is a prophecy that tells of a girl... they think she will change the world. For a long while they thought it would be for the better, but now they think she will destroy what they have worked for."

"Do they think that this girl is me?" My voice seeming to get raspier.

"They are careful with who knows what information. I thought maybe you were. The way the people around you hide you from everyone including yourself. The way he had people following you. It all seemed so suspicious." He pauses for a second. "I tried to intervene. If they ever thought it could be you, they don't any longer. He wouldn't have done what he did today if he still thought that."

"Tried to kill me?" I ask.

"No." He pauses again. "Inviting you to Friday."

"What is Friday." I ask unsure if I want to know the answer.

"Get dressed. We can talk more once you are comfortable." He turns away.

I dress carefully in the full outfit he gave me. Shorts, a soft t-shirt, and under garments. He returns with an arm full of supplies just as I painfully pull the shirt over my head. "Can you hop on the countertop here?" He points as he dumps his load on the opposite side of the sink. I make a weak attempt.

He gently helps me up by lifting me by my hips. He starts by changing the bandages on my thigh. The cuts have stopped bleeding, he seems satisfied at this as he applies ointment and new coverings. He looks at my arm and asks questions about the pain level. I tell him it is not as bad as it looks. One of his eyebrows lifts at that response. He asks about my head. Then hands me an ice pack when I say that is fine too. I hold it in place. It is shocking at first then the coolness slows the thumping pain. I shift and then flinch at the soreness in my ribs. I roll my eyes and say it is fine too. He lifts the hem of the shirt to check out the bruise there. This one really bothers him. He asks a lot more questions and even presses on it a couple of times. I try not to flinch away from him, but the pain is too much. He uses a long wrap bandage around my mid-section to hold an ice pack against it. The pain begins to subside.

"I can't do much about these, but we can cover them up." Talking about the marks on my neck.

I nod. With most of the worst sore spots finding a little relief, I can feel exhaustion setting in. He opens a few small compacts. Using a strange, shaped sponge, he gently applies a few layers of stuff that I do not see to my neck.

"The night I met you, you called me Janie." I am not sure why I have decided to start talking or why I chose to talk about this. He looks at me strangely. "At the roof top penthouse." I add for clarification. He still looks confused. "Remember, we left from there to the hotel bar. And you know…" I let the sentence fall away as I remember kissing him.

"The night we officially met. You were wandering around town." He explains.

"I guess it would maybe be the next time we met, after that one." I push him to remember.

He takes a deep breath. "I think you may have me confused with someone else who was there with you. By the time I got there you were slumped in a chair, barely coherent. Liam and Luke were there before I arrived. Liam let me know how bad it was getting so I went. I was only there shortly before I got you out." He pauses looking at my face for a reaction.

Was that kiss all in my head? I remember it feeling so real. His eyes are blue though, not green like I remember. Maybe it is all in my head. "I guess you are right. I remember you having green eyes that night. Maybe my brain is getting things mixed up." I admit aloud.

A thought he does not voice aloud crosses his features. "Could be." He says as he lifts my chin and continues the work on my neck. After a few more minutes of work, he puts down the sponge, steps back to admire his work, then helps me down from the counter.

I turn to the mirror to look. The marks on my neck are gone. No makeup lines or darker areas. It looks like fresh healthy skin. "Where did you learn to do that?"

"Lots of practice." He answers. "Why didn't you run?" He asks his question from earlier again.

"Where would I have gone, naked and hurt like I was?" I respond. He just looks at me expectantly. I look away from him. "I have nowhere to go. No one has ever helped me like this before. Not even Felicia." I admit. Shame washes over me.

He pulls my chin gently to look at him. "You should have run."

I am shocked at first as he wraps his arms around my shoulders, gentle and strong, he squeezes me. My head rests on his chest. He holds me there. Unsure of what to do I wrap my arms around his waist. I breath in the scent of him. I listen to his heartbeat. I feel... safe. *You idiot.* I scold myself.

Eight

Friday morning arrives. I wake up before the sun has a chance to blind me with her light. Anxiety pulses through my veins. Lane does not know what could be planned. He does not know what to warn me of exactly. He promises that he will not leave me alone and will try his absolute best not to let me get hurt. I do not feel reassured. All the sore places on my body still hurt and look worse today than when they happened, just days ago. It will get worse before it gets better. A saying Felicia used all the time when I lived with her.

Lane is sitting on the bed when I come out of the bathroom. A box sits next to him. His head is down. "I shouldn't take you there. I could come up with some kind of excuse of how you escaped."

I take a deep breath. He had this same conversation with himself last night. I did not have much to say then. I was so confused, and my mind was slow to think of responses.

Today though, I am refreshed. "Let's say that's what we do. I run off to hide somewhere. How long would I have before they come after me?"

"They may not." He looks up at me.

"Say they don't. How long will it be before I believe they aren't looking for me?" I say honestly.

I have thought about this. If I run now there is a chance they will come after me. There is also a chance they will not. What kind of life would I live always looking over my shoulder wondering if today is the day?

"I could go and let you know what they plan to do." He stands and starts pacing in thought.

"Then we would have an open line of communication that would make their pursuit of me easier if they so choose to take that route." I grab onto his arm, stopping him mid-step. "What is done is done." Another saying of Felicia's. "I say we go, face the music. Head on. He will see that I am a huge no body. I can apologize for distracting you. I can tell him that I will leave and never come back. We can both move on."

I am lying through my teeth. I am scared to death to face this man. I am scared for myself and Lane. I know that his threat is to somehow use me to hurt him. I do not want him to hurt me anymore. Deeper than that, I do not want me to be the reason that Lane is hurt.

What is wrong with you? You have a crush on this man who clearly has a whole trunk of issues of his own. You are willing to put yourself in harm's way for a man who kept you chained to a bed. I say these things to myself knowing this is exactly what Felicia would be saying to me right now.

"Jane, I can't do that." I look at him confused by what he is saying. He reads my face. "I don't think I can let you go." He watches my face. I cannot be sure, but I think he may also have a crush on me. This is not good. This is not healthy. "Jane." He says trying to get me to respond.

"I should get dressed. We should head out soon, right?" I ask him. Changing the subject.

He lets out a breath. "You are right." He hands me the box. "Your outfit."

He leaves the room. I do not watch him leave. I fear what I may see in his face. If he does not look back at me at all, I will be hurt because, irrationally, how dare he not look at me back? If he looks back at me the way I expect he will, I will be scared because, irrationally, how dare he fall for someone like me?

I have barely had time to accept being sober before I have somehow convinced myself to go with him. In the bigger picture, he has to go tonight no matter what decision is made. If not, that man will surely come looking for him. Yes, I do have the choice to not go. I could stay here, where the man would come looking for me anyway, or run away. I have done that before. I have nothing. I will end up back on the streets. It will not last long before I find my way to the pills or some other substance.

Lane genuinely wants me safe and sober. At this point I have no one else to trust. I dress and meet him in the living room. The dress is black. The skirt of it falls loosely to the floor. With a slit up the side of my good leg. The neck is cut in a deep 'v'. Fingerless gloves cover the bruise on my arm.

He looks me up and down. "It fits beautifully." He is dressed in a solid black suit with a blue shirt under the jacket. He pulls a box from his pocket. "This is for your neck."

I open the box. It is a cascading necklace, layered with black satin and strands of blue stones. He helps me put it on. A piece of the black satin wraps snug around my neck with alternating strands of blue stones and more black satin draping down in layers to my cleavage. The makeup hides the marks, but this will ensure they do not show through. I slide my feet in the black heels that are sitting near the door.

He joins me by the door. Takes a deep breath. "We could run together."

"Let's put this behind us first." This response puts him at ease. He may even be more nervous that I am. He takes my hand and leads the way to the car.

∞∞∞

Lane stops the car in front of a beautiful mansion. "Chalet Manor." He announces.

The name fits the house in an exact definition of the name. The long driveway to get here and the apparent never-ending wall of stone fence that follows the property as far as I can see. The roof is so wide it spreads far from the walls holding the structure. The circle of the driveway around us is lined with cars of all shapes, sizes, and models. Parked neatly apart.

He takes my hand and leads me up the stone stairway where large double doors stand as the entrance. He opens one side, and my breath catches at the view inside. A large staircase centers a great hallway. The hallway seems to stretch as far back as the property line seems to from outside. People are scattered in small groups through the space. A soft mummer of voices echoes in the air around me. A woman with a camera seemingly glued to her face dances through the groups. Snapping candid shots of the guests.

Lane hooks my arm in the crook of his elbow and walks as close to me as he can. He leans down to whisper, "Last chance. We can still run." I shake my head and squeeze his arm in reassurance.

Liam approaches us from a group hovering near the stairs. "Why did you bring it here?" He asks under his breath.

Lane does not respond. They share a look between them. Liam lets out a frustrated breath and walks back to his group. Tina. Tina loops her arm in his and smiles up at him. She does not even look toward me. I scan the room for Tracy.

Lane guides me as we make our way towards a large intimidating door. The walk feels long as we pass people. He smiles politely at each person that makes eye contact. He seems comfortable in this atmosphere. The people here know him. I feel completely out of place. I think to myself, *is it too late now? Yes, it is too late*, the large door swings open.

The room inside is wide and long. Chairs stand in perfect lines to each side of us in rows. The rows stop a few yards away from a long, ornate table with a line of thick, wide, throne-like seats facing back at the chairs we pass. Lane leads us to two chairs closest to the aisle in the front row. As we sit, I hear the room begin to fill with people. Liam passes in front of us with Tina still hooked in his arm. More people I do not know, fill more seats down our row. I glance around the room behind us. The large space is barely filled. Most people have chosen to sit in the first two rows of either side. Maybe totaling thirty people. The room could seat hundreds. Lane takes my hand and gently squeezes, reassuring me now.

A loud sound from behind the table quiets the room. Four men enter from the right and three women enter from the left. The white-haired man leads the line on the right. Followed by a middle aged, overweight, man and two frail looking old men. On the women's side a tall woman helps a frail woman to her seat, before taking her own. The last woman is… Felicia! I want to stand. To run to her. Lane puts a hand on my cheek and forces me to look at him. He shakes his head once and looks at me purposefully. I do not understand. Felicia is like my mother. If she knew what this man had done to me, she would not be sitting so calmly near him.

Reality crashes into my chest. A weight of clarity threatens to smother me. Heat climbs my spine and spreads through my shoulders. Lane puts both of his hands on either side of my face bringing me out of my own thoughts and back to now. I wonder if he knows what is happening in my brain. Does he know who Felicia is to me?

"I know." He whispers. My eyebrows crease together. He leans closer to me. "I wanted you to run. Do you want to run?" His voice is so low I can barely hear him.

I cannot run now. I must know what part Felicia

has played in this. I must know what part Tracy and Tina played. I have to know what is happening. I shake my head in his hands. He leans in even closer. His breath feels cool against my lips. Butterflies flutter through my belly. Hot fluttering wings.

"We all know why we are here today." Lane and I jump back from each other. The white-haired man begins the meeting, or whatever this is.

Luke crosses in front of us. He sneers at me, and then Lane, as he goes. Behind him, Tracy skips to keep up with his wide stride. She does not glance my way. They sit somewhere down this row.

"Our prophecies tell of a fallen angel who will come to us and change life as we know it. We once believed that she would come to change our life for the better. This is not so. Felicia," he gestures in her direction, "found this child when she first fell to our earth. She learned that she would not come here to lift us up, instead, she is here to take from us the very things that make each of us who we are."

Felicia stands, "Thank you, Carl." His name is Carl. Such an average name for someone so awful. "He is right. Somewhat. We have the child under control. We learn more about her every day. We will find a way to change what the prophecies say. They are just like rumors. We cannot trust what we do not fully understand. At this point, we can't be sure it is her that they speak of."

"That will be all Felicia." Carl says to her. He looks at her in a stern way. She sits in compliance. "We do in fact have this child under control. Liam." Lane squeezes my hand tightly in his. He tenses in his seat. Liam crosses the space between the front row and the table. Tina follows behind him carrying an old, tattered box. Lane shifts. "My son Liam has a gift. A talent that is strong as well as beautiful." He turns to Liam. "Does your gift speak to you now son?" Liam nods his chin once in response. "Lovely Tracy, will you?" He looks for Tracy in the seats. Tracy stands and turns to move in our direction. "Ladies and gentlemen, I present to you, our guest of honor." He says with a sneer. She stops in front of me and holds out her hand out, asking for mine.

Lane jumps up from his seat pulling me with him and away from Tracy. "No." He pulls me to his side. One of his arms wraps around me. The group of people react around the room with hushed whispers. "Liam, no." He says again.

Liam's head drops, he stares at the floor. Tracy grabs me by my free arm. Luke and two other men I do not recognize flank around Lane. He pulls me closer to him. His movement causes the group around us to react. The men over power him quickly and take him down easily. Tracy drags me to the table. I lock eyes with Felicia. Begging her to make this stop. She leans back in her chair and crosses her arms over her chest. She stares me down. I do not understand what she expects of me.

"Lie down on the table." Tracy pulls my attention back. I do not understand what she is asking me. So, she asks again and pushes me to the table.

I do as she says. The wounds of my body are too fresh to risk adding more because of a bad attitude. I encouraged Lane to come here. We have to face… I cut off my own thoughts. Those were Felicia's words. I stretch out on the table in front of the people seated in the large chairs. Carl has taken his seat. My head rests in front of his spot. Tracy passes the box to Liam. He sets it to the side, opens it, and begins setting its contents out on the table around my head.

From where I left him Lane yells, "Liam, what are you doing? Don't do this." He is begging him.

I watch Liam's face flinch. He regains his composure. Hands come down hard on my arms and legs. Pinning me to the table. I hold back the whimper of the sore spots being jarred. I cannot see the faces or bodies attached to the other ends of the hands on me.

Liam leans close to my ear. "I'm sorry." He does not look me in the eye.

He pushes my head to the side. Carl does not have a problem holding eye contact with me. I hear a strange buzz of a machine click to life. Liam presses harder on my face. The buzzing sound grows louder. Then I feel the first of the burn. I close my eyes and hold back any emotion. He runs the buzzing machine in some kind of formation across my face. The burning seems to spread from my nose to my hairline, across my cheek bone, and down to my chin. A tattoo. He is tattooing my face. Probably branding me.

The burning pain continues. The pain threatens to break the careful hold I have on my self-control. I mentally lock myself away. I do not struggle against the hands pinning me to the table. I do not cry at the searing pain across my face. The heat of the pain mixes with the heat of my anger. It threatens to overthrow my control. There are too many of them here for me to have a chance.

Whether it is a chance to escape or fight, I will lose. I close my eyes and wait for it to end.

I do not realize when the hands guide me to sitting up. I do not comprehend when they lead me away from the table. His voice brings me back. I am in his arms.

"Jane. Jane, look at me." I do as he says. The whites of his eyes are red. The blue of his irises shimmer in contrast. "Jane." He says my name like an apology. I can hear all the things he means to say in that one word. He is sorry. He failed me. He feels betrayed by the people in this room too.

The heat of the pain rushes back to me. The mental restrictions I had in place fall away. I cannot speak over the burn pulsing across my face. The heat in my shoulders turns to fire. I cannot tell if it is painful. It scares me. Like a fire is threatening to explode from my body and this tattoo has given it a line of exit. Lane is watching my face fearfully. Something else is happening. He latches his arms around me. The sounds of the room make their way to my consciousness.

Two men are pulling Lane's arms away from me. Tracy has looped her arm around my waist. Pulling me back to the audience chairs. They win. We are separated. A chair has been brought to where Liam waits. The men around Lane force him to sit in it. He undoes the buttons down his shirt silently.

I watch as Tina carries a bowl and cloth to Liam. He uses them to wipe across Lane's chest. As he does, makeup smears away. Revealing tattoos. So many that all the cleaned area is covered in them.

"Sit down." Tracy orders me. Unsure of what else to do, I sit. She sits in Lane's empty seat beside me. "This is happening because of you." She whispers.

I do not respond to her. I do not look at her. My eyes are fixed on Lane, who is looking at me. His features are tight. The buzz from Liam's tool starts up. Lane does not flinch when it touches his skin.

"You were out of control," she continues, "and set things in motion much sooner than we anticipated. Felicia is the only one who knew that you would get involved with one of the sons. We were stupid not to listen to her, but you know how crazy she can sound sometimes. Plus, you have never shown interest in any man before. How were we to know you would do something so stupid?"

I have never felt this negative energy coming from her. She is my best friend. Was my best friend. Or so I thought. Carl's voice echoes through the room.

He seems to be midsentence, "…a gift that will let us properly track this angel, this curse. Every single one of us here believes in Him. He will come, soon now, I can feel it. We will present her to Him as a gift. He has promised to ensure that we keep our powers. Our powers will grow stronger under his guidance. Our numbers increase yearly, our kind will soon lead on every piece of land this earth has." The small crowd around us cheers and claps.

He continues. I stop listening. This is some kind of strange cult. At first, I thought this 'Him' he was speaking of was some kind of leader, but as his words continue about serving this person and doing his bidding, I think now it is some sort of God that he has led these people to believe in. He seems to think that I am the key to getting this God of his to give him more power. Too bad I am not this 'fallen angel', I cannot be. I am a nobody in a room full of people.

Do Tracy and Tina believe him? Why are they here? Felicia, too? The heat in my body dissipates. The burn of my cheek is the only heat left.

Nine

Lane pulls his shirt and jacket back into their right places. Liam gathers his tools. Carl stands, as if to add a closing speech. The door, Lane and I entered, slams open with a loud, echoing thud. The room goes silent. A sharp tap, tap, tap of high heels against the hardwood floor moves quickly down the aisle.

Carl welcomes her, "Kate! My love welcome home. I have something special for you."

"Carl, sit down!" Her voice is strong and beautiful. She stops walking when she reaches the table. She does not look back at us in the audience. She looks up and down the table. "Pacha, get poor Edna out of here." Pacha, the younger of the two women that I do not know, stands, and helps Edna, the frail old woman, from her chair and towards the way they came in. "Felicia I am glad to see you. I expect we have a lengthy conversation to have."

Felicia nods sucking her lips together, as if she has something else, she wants to say. She holds the words back. She follows Pacha and Edna.

Kate looks down the other end of the table. "Supay, Brock, and Dean. How lovely it is to see you all. You will have to fill me in on what the pleasure of your company means. Not here." She holds a hand to stop them from talking. They all stand and leave the room. She spins on her heel and faces us. "The rest of you can take advantage of the lovely meal being served in the dining room. If you are not my sons, you may exit." She watches the small crowd begin to shuffle out of their seat. Her eyes stop on me as I stand to leave. "What is this?" Her heels tap as she crosses the short distance to stand in front of me. I glance to Lane. "Liam." She barks.

"He was only doing what I asked of him." Carl defends him.

"Did you agree to this?" She asks me.

I do not respond, unsure of what may happen if I open my mouth. My silence seems to be answer enough for her. Most of the room has emptied out. Tracy and Tina have stood, but hover together near the aisle.

"Can I help you ladies with something?" Kate asks them.

Tracy responds, "We are here with Luke and Liam."

Kate looks around the room in disbelief. "Leave." She shoos them with a wave of her hand. She gently takes my hand. "Sit." I hear Tina huff.

"We needed a better solution for tracking her. He will come for her soon enough." Carl is saying to Kate as she crosses the space again. This time stopping in front of Lane. He is standing, his eyes on me.

Kate notices. "Did you bring her here?" She asks him. His eyes drop to the floor. She looks to Liam who is now standing next to Lane. "Did your senses tell you to do this, or Carl?"

"Both." He answers curtly. His eyes drop to the floor too.

"Where is Luke?" She glances around to see him still sitting in his seat.

"This time, I have nothing to do with any of this." He says defensively. Proud of himself, he smiles at her.

She takes a deep breath. "Well, since we have all of our clan leaders in one place, we may as well take advantage of that." She looks at Carl, "I am assuming you have made arrangements for them to all stay here, at least one night."

"Of course. I have so much to fill you in on. He is coming soon." Carl says enthusiastically. He almost claps his hands in display of his joy. He folds his fingers together. The look on Kate's face is clearly not amused by him.

She does not say anything else to him. She turns to Liam, "Does she understand what that tattoo means?" He shakes his head and looks at the floor again. She lets out a huff. "You boys will stay here until further notice. Do not cross me." Liam and Luke leave down the aisle together. Lane starts towards me. "She can stay with you if that is what you want. Is she clean?" He nods at her once. "It is your choice then. Keep her here with you or send her out." She pats his shoulder as he passes her and collects me.

He does not speak until we exit the room. Laughter, and the clinking of glasses, floats from somewhere far down the hall. I tense at the thought of having to be around anymore people.

"Do you think you can walk upstairs, a lot of stairs?" He asks me.

I nod. We scale the first set of stairs. He keeps my hand in his, and his other free hand on my lower back. I am satisfied with myself when we reached the top. Only to be led to another set of stairs. I take a deep breath and he helps more this time. My thigh is the one protesting the walk. The heels are probably not helping. He guides me through a couple of hallways before finally stopping in front of a large set of wooden double doors.

He opens one side and guides me through. Inside is the biggest bedroom I have ever seen. This house has the biggest everything I have ever seen. There is a huge bed in the center of this room. With tall, broad furniture for storage, placed around the room. Through an arch way is a sitting area with a love seat and lounge chair that sits in front of a walk-in closet the size of my apartment. Back in the bedroom area a door leads to a massive on-suite. Equipped with a jetted tub and separate, large, walk in shower.

"This is your house, your bedroom?" I ask. Mesmerized by the size of everything.

"Well, I haven't stayed here in a long time." He looks at me. "Yes, this is my family's house." He answers. "Make yourself comfortable." He disappears into the walk-in closet.

I start to rub my hands against my face. The pain jerks them away. A small round mirror hanging on the wall reflects my face back to me. I move closer, slowly. It is not as big as it felt while getting it. It is pretty. Seems to be well executed to my untrained eye. A swirling of lines that dance in the space of my cheek bone.

He clears his throat as he returns with a small box and stack of fresh clothes. "I can have better clothes sent up tomorrow. I figured these would do for tonight." He passes me a t-shirt and a pair of his linen pants. "They are the smallest things I could find in there."

I glance back in the mirror. "What does it mean?"

"It is more about what it can do." He answers. "I think you should see something before I tell you more about it. I will need to shower." I nod at him. He does not move, "Would you help me?"

"Shower?" I ask in confusion.

"Yes." He looks at me expectantly. "Just to help me get this stuff off. It has been a long while since I have made sure I have gotten all of it. I won't strip all the way down." He clarifies.

I think back to the wiping away of makeup from his chest. "Yes." I answer.

I follow him to the bathroom. He strips down to his briefs. Tattoos start at the top of his feet and move up his legs. A mod podge of shapes and designs. They continue up his back, until makeup starts to cover them. He starts the water in the shower.

He turns his back to me. I strip down to the panties and bra that he gave me to wear under the dress. They cover more than some swimwear I have seen, but I still feel exposed. He does not turn back to look at me. He climbs in the shower, leaving the door open in invitation. He faces the stream from the shower head. I step in behind him. He passes me a cloth and a bar of soap. He lathers up a cloth of his own and begins massaging his forehead and cheeks. I lather the one in my hand.

    I start high on his back. The makeup washes away easily. His skin comes to life. Images and shapes cover the expanse of his back. I move to his shoulders and down his arms. When his muscles shift the images follow, dancing a slow waltz. Thin lines overlap thick lines. Curves and corners. Not any tattoo designs I have seen on other guys. No barbed wire or tribal shapes. No recognizable shapes like animals or letters. Delicate lines, bold lines, heavily shaded areas, and some faded. Beautifully mend together.

    He slowly turns, my eyes follow the shapes as they continue. His chest is made of designs that mirror each other on either side. Aside from the newest one added today. The new ink stands out in comparison to the others around it. The shapes of it may even be an exact replication of the one on my face.

    A single, not tattooed straight line, about a centimeter wide separates the two sides. The line without tattoos gets thinner as it moves up his neck and separates the two halves of his face all the way to his hair line. His top lip and the area around his eyes are the only other areas with untouched skin. I get lost in the designs as I look at his face. Hours and hours had to be spent designing all of these.

    Caught up in the magic of watching his skin change before my eyes, I trail my fingertips along a straight line down the right side of his neck. Chill bumps raise on his skin behind my touch. I jerk my hand away and step back realizing that at some point I have moved close enough to him that our chests were nearly touching. His body is rigidly stiff.

"I'm sor…," I start to say as I look away from his body.

He stops me. Gently, he cradles my face in both of his hands. Pulling me to look at him. "You never need to apologize to me. Not after what I have put you through."

He starts to drop his hands from my face. Maybe it is the tension between us. Maybe it is the pain clouding my judgement. Before I can stop myself, I grab his face and pull him to me. The heat in my belly pushes me to close the small distance between us. My lips press against his. The heat turns to fire. His lips feel like ice against mine. Not like the kiss from before. Not a primal need to attack him.

A territorial need. *Mine*. My mind growls.

Ten

I wake with a jump. A dream that has haunted me for as long as I can remember. There are no people in this dream. No words. Just a sound of a beating drum getting faster. A clay like substance that pulses with the beat of the sound. Only this time the clay is fire. A fire that pulses and stretches. Reaching out to me. I have never understood why this dream causes me to feel such fear.

I am alone in his bed. He slept on the sofa in the dressing room, or so he called it. The two of us had dinner in here alone. We talked some. Mostly about his tattoos. Liam has only ever tattooed him, before the one I now have on my cheek. He tried to help me understand how they use them to communicate. Liam can manipulate the way they feel on his skin. He can make them tingle or tickle, he explained to me. Even make them hurt if the issue is urgent. They have been doing this long enough, and Lane has enough tattoos, that they can practically hold full conversations between them.

All that anyone else knows is that Liam can always find Lane. No matter how far apart they are. They have kept the rest a secret. Carl is hopeful that this tattoo will make it so that Liam will always know where I am. It sounds like it did not work though. Liam claims that it is not the same with my tattoo. They have not decided what to tell Carl yet.

A light succession of taps on the door makes me jump. I sit up to see Lane still asleep, stretched out on the sofa, in the other room. I stare at the door considering what to do. I decide to ignore it and hope whoever is on the other side goes away. The knob turns. The dark skin of her fingers pushes through the small crack. She pulls her fingers toward herself, beckoning me to go to her. I quietly slide from the bed and tiptoe to the hallway. Felicia is looking at me with a pain filled gaze.

My emotions go on a rampage in my mind. Trying to decide how I feel about her now. "Hi, Felicia." Is what my lips let out.

"I know you distrust me now. It was my job to keep that boy away from you. He is in there isn't he?" She looks back at the door like she can see right through it. "Yeah, he's in their all right." She smacks her hand across her own forehead. "Come, let's have some tea."

I hesitate to follow. "I think I would rather wait for Lane." I say with caution.

She takes a deep breath and lets it out slowly. "I can't undo what's been done, but I sure as hell am not going to leave you without at least telling you what I know." She continues walking. I look back to the door of the bedroom before finally deciding to follow her.

She seems smaller in this big house. She always seemed so tall and strong in her tiny shack. I follow her down one set of stairs and through another great hall before she turns into a room. The lights are on low. There are sofas with coffee tables separating them. A few tables with large chairs pushed under them. An entire room clearly used only for drinking tea. The main décor is floral, and each table has empty snack towers standing in the center. She motions for me to sit on the first sofa, as she goes over to a countertop. I do not watch her as she pours the tea, but I can hear the gentle clanks of silver against porcelain and smell the bitter aroma of a dark tea. She brings two glasses, already having added the sugar. For a moment I am taken back to her shack. Dirty and small as it was, drinking tea at her small table is the most home-like feelings I have.

She jumps right in when she gets herself comfortable on the sofa opposite me. "Now, simple as my mind is, what Carl says is true. The prophecies are real. I cannot say that his interpretation of them is correct, but I have read them myself. These people are dangerous. They have strong powers and some of them like to abuse that power."

"You mean like mind reading." I suggest, trying not to blow any cover for Lane.

"Mind reading seems small in the greater picture of what they can do." She sips her tea. "Some can control things around them like water and air. Some can change the shapes of their bodies. I am sure there are many more with many different skills. Their kind has stayed hidden. Carl does not like this. He wants to rule over people. Kate doesn't like it either, but she would rather take a more political direction."

"Why have you not told me about this before?" I ask.

"Carl is sure you are the fallen angel he talks about. I knew from the moment you walked down my street that you were special. I do not know about the fallen angel part. They weren't around for your teen years." She laughs at the tease. "I promised him I would handle you if he and his sons stayed away from you. I made sure you had good friends and lived as best a life I could offer." She pauses for a long time. Lost in some thought she does not add words to. "Things have changed now. He is back. Carl will do whatever he thinks may please Him."

"Who is this 'He'? I thought at first everyone was talking about Carl. But then, he started saying it too."

"Dean is the only one that has ever spent any time around Him. He is the only one who knows His name. The elders have forbidden anyone from knowing it. He is dangerous and the elders fear Him. Carl worships Him. I imagine he is probably just a man with a strong gift that he has used to abuse others." She stops in thought again.

"How do you fit in all of this?" I ask her.

"I'm just an old woman from the swamp land, who fell in love with a child that needed a mother." She looks at me. I believe her. All of me believes her. If harm comes my way because of her, it was not her intention. She finishes her tea. "Now, you better get. As much as I hate it, he will be looking for you soon."

"The man with no name?" I ask. Saying it aloud makes me feel silly. A 'man with no name', are we living in a child's bedtime story?

"Ha! I'd be so lucky." She laughs. I do not understand her. She shakes her head at me. "That stupid boy upstairs."

"Felicia," I stop her from leaving, "did you know about the pills?"

Her head drops. "There are some things from this world that I couldn't keep away from you." She lets out a long breath.

"Tracy? Tina? Did they know?" I ask.

She looks at me with her dark eyes. "Be careful who you trust. Each person has their own agenda in mind first." She warns me. She has told me this many times before. It was her response when I got my first job and what she said after I put the deposit on the apartment.

I walk out of the room feeling more confused than when I entered. She said she was going to tell me all that she knew. Is this it? People with magic powers surround me and that I should not trust anyone.

Eleven

I retrace my steps back upstairs. Careful not to get lost in the maze of this place. At the top of the staircase, I round the corner. A body coming from that direction slams into me. My ribs recoil and a sharp pain wakes up the healing bruise. I know it is Lane before he starts apologizing. I can sense when he is close. I cannot explain it, I just know in the deep areas of my mind, when he is near me.

"I'm sorry. I was not expecting you to wake up before me. Did I hurt you?" His words spill out in a rush.

"The ribs are still a bit sore." I tell him. "Felicia woke me up. I didn't want to bother you." I explain as we make our way back to his room.

In the room he paces, rubbing his hands together, weaving his fingers in and out. I place a hand on his arm to ease his tension. "What did she say?" He asks.

I give the cliff notes on what we talked about. "I think she just wants what's best for me." I tell him as I also try to convince myself it is true.

This seems to satisfy him. He answers a knock on the door. A large cart is pushed into the room. The person who pushed it in ducks back out quickly. The cart if filled with clothes. "This should be everything you need. If you have special requests, just let me know, I will get it for you." He pushes the cart into the walk-in closet.

"I can't accept this." I tell him.

"Well, you need clothes. Ones that actually fit." He looks at me still in his t-shirt and linen pants. "You don't have to keep them. You can just leave them here when we go."

I nod in agreement at that. I will need clothes. Going back to my place to stock up is long passed the ability to do so. I push away the thoughts about what could be left of my stuff. I pick out an outfit for today. We both freshen up and get dressed.

He starts to apply the makeup to his face. "Do you have to wear that?" I ask.

He looks at me in shock at my question. He considers it and then relaxes. A smile lifts one side of his lips. "Kate says it makes the people around me more comfortable if I cover them up."

"That may be true around strangers, but the people here, they know you right? They are your family." I say to him.

He looks at the sponge in his hand for a while before deciding to put it away. He wipes off the makeup that he had started to apply. He turns back to me, wraps his arms around my waist, and looks down into my eyes. His eyes are bright blue in this light and in contrast to the dark color of the tattoos. The curved lines of tattoos shape his cheek bones. Straight lines follow the squareness of his jawline.

"Your way it is then." He says to me teasingly. He kisses my nose.

I pull away from him. To ease the hurt that tries to wrinkle his features, I spin around and say, "If I have to parade around here in this fancy mansion wearing fancy clothes, then the least you could do is not hide behind a mask."

His smile widens at my tease. Something about him changes then. Not a bad thing, not even a big thing, I cannot put my finger on it, but something changes slightly.

∞∞∞

The house is busy with movement. A delicious smell fills the main hall. My stomach rumbles with hunger. We pass people I do not recognize. They politely smile then continue working. I assume they are housekeepers. Dusting and arranging things that already look clean and perfectly positioned.

Felicia hurries out of one door and passes by us. "Everyone to the dining room. Good morning sweet child." She says to me. "Lane." She smiles at him with wide eyes. She passes through another door.

Lane leads the rest of the way to the dining room. My jaw drops at the sight of the room. It is long and narrow like a hallway. A single table spans the entire length of the room. There could be enough seating for forty people to dine comfortably. Liam and Kate are the only two others in here right now. Liam approaches us while

Kate is busy with setting the table.

"Are you sure?" Liam asks Lane in a low voice.

Lane looks at me and smiles. "Yes, I am sure." I assume they have already had a conversation mentally. Or however those tattoos work.

Liam looks at me. His smile fades. "I really am sorry. About how it all went down."

"I think I am starting to understand." I answer truthfully. For some reason I do not blame him. After Lane explained what the tattoos are capable of and Felicia mentioned superhuman powers, I imagine things could be much worse.

A wailing cry interrupts us. "What are you doing?" Kate cries from the other end of the table. "No. We have talked about this." She says more severely. I glance around the room trying to figure out if someone else entered. "Lane, go now, before anyone else comes down. Breakfast will be done soon."

Liam tucks his hands in his pockets and backs away from us. She is moving our way. It is something *we* have done. Lane wraps one arm around me.

"Kate, I don't understand what the problem is." He says to her.

I think steam may be coming out of her ears. The room fills with her anger. "Go cover it up now!"

The *tattoos*. She is angry that he is not covering them with makeup. I glare up at him. He did not tell me that Kate would be this upset if he did not cover them. My frustration shifts. Why would she be so cross about this?

"I don't think I will today." He tells her. "Besides, breakfast will be served soon."

"It makes everyone uncomfortable seeing you like that. I thought you agreed that you did not like being read like an open book. Here you are, your story written all over you." She points to a specific mark somewhere on his arm. He tucks that arm behind himself. He feels... shame.

"I think they are beautiful." I say quietly. Trying to calm them both.

Lane gazes down at me. The shame that he feels fades some and he squeezes me closer to his side. Kate lets out a loud huff of frustration. The tattoo on my own cheek tingles like a cool breeze passes over it leaving chill bumps behind in the lines of the tattoo. The sensation is strange.

Liam starts coughing like he swallowed a drink wrong. "That was intense." He says after catching most of his breath. Kate stomps away.

Luke comes in next with Carl at his heels. I cannot help myself from cowering away from him as he passes us by. He makes a strange 'hmph' sound as he goes. Luke stares. Lane leads me to a seat and takes the one next to me. Tina and Tracy make their way in. Chatting quietly together. Kate finally sits as Felicia comes in. She sits directly across from me and winks. Pacha moves slowly for Edna's sake. They find seats. The three other men Dean, Supay, and Brock, I do not know which one is which, come in the middle of some debate. I think they are talking about flying. Others walk in too. People I do not recognize. Servers push in carts filled with covered dishes. Each person at the table gets one. The servers take the covers and leave. Chatter rises as we all eat. All the people that were in the meeting yesterday seem to be here again today. *Are there enough rooms in this house for every one of these people to have stayed the night?*

The tension in the room begins to thicken the air around me. Felicia kicks Lane under the table. "They are talking about you, boy." She gestures with her fork down to where the elders have chosen to sit. "They don't like your real face." She grins like she enjoys the torment Lane is causing them.

Lane grins back. "I don't think they liked me before. What is one more thing to add to their list?" His lips lift in a half smile. The light in his eyes shine.

My cheek catches a chill. Again, only in the lines of the tattoo. Liam starts choking, again. He pushes away from the table and excuses himself. "I'm sorry." He says as he leaves. I think he means it for me in particular.

Lane pushes back. "I am going to check on him. Are you ok here?" He asks me.

Felicia answers for me, "She is fine."

He squeezes my thigh and jogs after Liam. Butterflies with wings of fire dance in my belly. Others start to leave. Carl glares at me as he passes. The fire fizzles out. I pick at the food left on my plate. The room is mostly empty. The oldest of the three men makes his way toward the exit. He stops behind me.

He breathes in deeply. "Mmm, I smell the death on you." He continues to leave.

I stare across the table at Felicia who is smiling at

his back. She notices the bewilderment on my face. "That is Supay. He has a special relationship with death." She says it as if we are talking about a hobby he does well. "Oh, calm down. He isn't saying you are going to die." She adds when my face does not change. She pushes away from the table. "Let's go find the others." She ends the conversation before I can even start it.

I follow her out. Everything is strange here. Her and Lane talked as if they have known each other a long time. Supay smelled me. Felicia did not act as if that should bother me. What did he mean by smelling death on me? Anger creeps up my spine. The chance to word my questions to Felicia washes away with a wave of emotions filling the air of the main hall we are walking through.

I run to follow the emotions to the room where the meeting was held. The chairs and table are all in the same positions as before. Carl is standing in the open space between the table and audience chairs.

He is yelling, "We are going to allow him to walk around here like this? With his pet? We marked her so she wouldn't have to stay here!"

"She is safer here than out on the streets." Liam suggests. His eyes find me still in the shadows near the entrance.

"He would rather us have her here. If he comes like you say he will." Kate tries to reason.

"She should have her own say. You don't have any proof that she is the one." Lane challenges.

Carl's face contorts in response. The air around him seems to shiver in response to his anger. The tingle traces my tattoo. The heat of my own anger rises. Liam starts chocking. Carl barrels between everyone else slamming his body into Lane's. My anger spikes up my neck. I run the short distance of the aisle. Liam stands in front of me.

"You should leave." He warns. He coughs again.

I ignore him. I push past him and then Luke. Kate is standing over Carl and Lane. Yelling at them to stop. Her face changes when she sees me. "Everyone, stop!" She roars.

Her voice finally breaks through the commotion. She keeps her eyes on me. Carl begins to laugh getting to his feet. Lane stands holding his hands out like he is approaching a wild animal.

"Jane. Why don't we take a walk?" Kate says to me cautiously. I feel my head snap in her direction as she talks. "Lane. Stay back." She warns him.

"Sara told us this would happen." Carl laughs louder. "She's going to blow!"

My body is tense. My breathing is jagged. The heat of my anger is consuming me. I want to scream at Carl. I want to kick him. I want everyone to stop looking at me like they are right now.

"Luke now." Kate barks.

Luke scoops me up in his arms and is running faster than I have ever seen someone move. My brain spins. The heat inside me pulses. He drops me on cool, green grass. I cannot stop it this time. The heat only grows. Tears sting at my eyes. My body rocks. Breathing becomes difficult. The air that goes in feels like ice stinging all the way into the depth of my lungs. The air that comes out is thick like smoke. The earth below me starts to shake and crack. The grassy area splits apart. An orange haze covers my vision. An explosion goes off with a loud rumble.

Then everything around me is wet. I am drowned in water. My world goes black and silent.

Twelve

A ball of fire dances before my face. Slowly it starts stretching and shrinking. My hands reach out for it. I try to stop myself. The stretching and shrinking gets faster, and a beating drum grows louder with each passing second. My hands reach closer to the fire. I try to make them stop. Force myself to drop them back by my sides. They continue forward until the fire jumps on my palms. I sit up screaming.

The room is dark. I can feel that I am in a bed. The fire is gone. Only the remnants of the nightmare in the shadow of my mind. Something stumbles as it moves closer to me. I shrink back. The fear of the nightmare still pulsing through my veins.

"Are you all right?" A breathless voice says from the object moving closer. *Lane.* It is only Lane. I let out a breath. "Jane, are you ok?" He asks again.

"Bad dream." I mutter.

"Do you want me to lay with you for a little while?"

I start to say yes, but then I remember what really happened. I remember all the fear, and anger pulsing through my body. I remember the fire. "I don't know if you should." I warn. He reaches out for my hand. I snatch it away. "Don't touch me." Hurt, rejection, and fear swirl through the room. "No, I am sorry. I didn't mean it like that."

He does not say anything. He does not have to. I can feel his emotions. I have been feeling emotions of others since… well, I do not know. I think when I started getting sober. I drop my head in my hands. I feel the cold of my tattoo under my fingertips. The door to the hall bursts open.

Between coughs, Liam's voice comes through the darkness to us, "Lane, where are you? What is happening?"

"We are ok." Lane answers.

Liam flips on the light. "I think we should all have a talk."

"Not now." Lane says. "It is the middle of the night."

"Yes, now. Not here though." I say quietly.

Jealousy fills the space between the three of us. Liam says, "Stop that." He coughs some more. "I don't even understand what is happening. It is like your emotions are attacking me. I promise I will never tattoo you again no matter how strong the urge is."

"That is not me." I jump down from the bed. "Where can we go to talk?"

"I know a place." Lane answers.

"Ah man." Liam huffs.

They lead me outside. Across the grounds in the

back of the house. We pass a strange black hole in the ground. "You." Liam says. Lane huffs. Jealousy fills the air stronger. Liam coughs. We walk a long time before finally we stop near some hedges. There is a water fountain and some benches. In the dark it is hard to tell much more.

"No one comes out here, not even during daylight." Lane says.

"Before this conversation gets going, I need you both to remember that whatever she feels, I feel times ten." Liam announces.

"I can feel the emotions of people near me." I admit. *Confusion.* "Sometimes, I can even see it." I add as I watch the waves of it move through the space between us.

"I was relieved when it looked like the tattoo wasn't going to work between you two the same way." Lane admits. "Now I hate that it does work."

"The urge to tattoo you wasn't so strong that I couldn't hold back. I was excited that I even had the urge with someone else." Liam admits. "Now though, tattooing you was too much. It may kill me." He adds the last part for dramatic effect. But I think we all believe it.

"We cannot tell anyone how strong you are." Liam says urgently, like we are running out of time.

"I don't even know how strong I am." I admit.

"The strongest." They say in unison.

Lane leans forward in his seat. Fear moves the air around him. "He is going to come this time."

I now understand the 'he' they are talking about is

probably bad news. At least for me. "What will he want?" *Fear.* My own. Liam does not cough. The tattoo gets the chill bumps. "That's me."

Liam looks at me. "So, when it is other people's emotions that's when I get attacked?"

"I think it may be because I feel attacked by the other emotions. Especially strong ones." I respond.

Lane controls his jealousy slightly better than before. "So, you can produce fire and feel emotions of other people. What else can you do?"

Stifling the emotion mentally does not stop it from leaking in his words. "I was not aware I could do any of this before the last few days."

"That isn't what is important right now." Liam interjects. "That you can do anything will be answer enough for them. They will all start fighting over which side you should be on."

"What side is the right one?"

Lane's eyebrows furrow as he stares down his brother. "She shouldn't have to choose a side." His features soften, turning to me. "You should be able to make your own choice about what happens next."

Liam thinks for a moment. "Out of the elders that are here now I can tell you what each of them think." I nod at him to continue. "Supay and his clan believe that the fallen angel will come to the earth to grant them more power and strengthen the ones they have. Carl and Brock believe that she is here to take away the powers but, if they can turn her over to Him, He will stop that from happening. Finally, Felicia does not believe that any one person has either of those abilities. Her spiritual beliefs tell her that something is definitely wrong, but they don't give her the answers either."

Lane adds, "That is why that group has the smallest number of votes on her side. People don't trust what they can't see."

I want to know more about the powers other people have but knowing would make all this more real. What I did scares me. No person should have the power to explode. The earth shattered under me. If someone is coming to take it all away, I think I would choose that side if given the decision right now.

I look between them. They must have opinions on this too. "What do you guys think?"

They look at each other. The air between them ripples. "We will do what we can to protect you." Lane answers. My cheek tingles. "For now, let us keep our circle small. No one else can know what all you can do. Not even Felicia." He says pointedly.

"I don't even know what that means. I am in no hurry to expand that confusion." I think for a moment. "No one knows where these powers come from or why?"

"Only the elders." Liam answers.

Lane explains. "We think that maybe they keep it all secret because they can't agree on a definite answer. They are all looking for proof."

"What makes them elders?" I ask.

"A group of them were friends years ago. They

discovered each of them had powers. They started researching everything they could. Dean was the one who discovered Him. The others did not like his answer and swore him to secrecy until he could prove it. They have been arguing ever since." Lane tells me.

"Kate wants to go all Professor X on the situation." Liam sees my confusion and explains, "She thinks that people with gifts like ours shouldn't be hidden. That they should be trained and learn to live normal lives that include the gifts. She has spent years documenting all of us. When we aquired our powers, how often they are used, she even takes pictures of every new tattoo I put on Lane."

This idea intrigues me. Would it be possible? I have barely known about this for a day, and I have my doubts. If there are people willing to hurt others to get their way and they have these kinds of abilities, what would a normal life look like for those who do not have these things? Would people without these powers ever trust in people who can burn down cities with a thought or read minds? I can see where this is much to debate.

Thirteen

The sun starts to rise and feeling very unaccomplished, the three of us head back inside. Lane and I get ready in his room. "You didn't want me to touch you earlier." I try to look for the right answer for him. "Liam says you are scared of yourself."

I swallow the lump in my throat. "If Luke were not as fast as he is, I could have killed everyone. I couldn't stop myself."

He pulls me close and kisses me. His cool lips instantly set a fire in my belly. I pull back, "Just like that I think I could catch on fire." I try to smile. The fear of this reality is too much to hide though.

"That, before, was from anger and fear. This, now, is different." He pulls me back to him. "You won't hurt me." He kisses me again. Deeper.

I relax into his arms. The fire burns inside me. That primal instinct that he is mine consumes my mind. Our clothes are off before I can even think about it. He lifts me by my thighs, and I wrap my legs around his waist. He moves us to the bed. Every part of him feels like ice against me. He finds my center and pushes inside. His ice fills me everywhere. The tension cools away. All I can feel is him. All I can smell is him. All I can taste is him. We find a rhythm. His breathing gets thick and heavy. The burning in my belly rises. I use my body to flip us over so I can be above him. My climax gets closer. Small moans escape my throat. He sits up, holding me to him. Meeting my every movement. He covers his mouth over mine to stifle the next series of moans coming from both of us. My body pulses as his releases fresh ice. I wrap my arms and legs around him and bury my hot face into his cold neck. Our bodies calm together. Our heart beats slow against each other. My body shudders. I am freezing cold.

"Do you need a blanket?" He asks while turning us around to find one. The blankets behind us are covered in a thin layer of ice.

"I don't think those blankets are going to do much warming right now." I laugh lightly.

"Was that you?" He asks.

I look at him, "That was you." He looks again at the blankets. "Have you never done that before?"

A banging on the door has us scrambling away from each other. "Go start the shower." He tells me as he finds his pants and jumps to put them on.

I rush to turn on the water. Once it is going, I lean against the door to listen.

"Lane!" Kate shouts from the hallway.

"I'm coming." He responds to her. I hear the door to the bedroom open hard. "Kate! Whoa!"

"No, you did not! What were you thinking?" She yells.

"Kate, get out. We will be down in a bit." He says calmer now.

"Is that ice? Was that you?" Her voice grows higher with each word.

"We aren't talking about this now. I'm not even dressed." He tells her.

"What difference does that make?" She nearly squeals at him. "You are walking around with your tattoos all out. Why not roam the halls without a shirt on?"

"You are my mother and I'm not a kid anymore." He gets a little louder.

"Oh, now all of a sudden I'm your mother." Her voice mocking.

"Dammit. I'm not doing this now." Frustration is now clear in his tone of voice. I cannot feel it through the door though.

"Oh, yes, you are." It sounds like she stomps her foot. "You have to understand what you are doing. She is a bad influence on you. That could come with real trouble."

"We have it under control, Kate." He responds.

I cannot hear anything through the door anymore. Either they have walked away or are now talking too low. I get in the shower and start the motions of washing. A little while passes before Lane comes in. He gets in the shower with me. He takes my face in his hands and kisses me.

"Are we in trouble?" I ask when he pulls away.

"No, not really. Kate is just shocked." He assures

me.

Once we are clean, we stand together in front of the sink. Most of the bruises on my neck have healed. The one on my ribs does not hurt to touch anymore but looks a nasty brown and yellow. I dress and rake a comb through my hair. I hop up on the countertop to watch him as he finishes getting ready.

I look at the tattoos covering his face. Following the maze of lines from his brow to his chin. Then continue down his neck to his, still bare, chest. Stopping where his pants sit loosely on his hips. I imagine the stories that each piece may tell. I wonder where they started.

I ask, "Which one was first?"

He hesitates a moment before finally holding out his left wrist. A single, thick, straight line starts at the thumb side of his inner wrist and stops at the pinky side. "I was sixteen. Liam was twelve. It was a difficult age for me. I had tried to take my own life. Over something that seems so small now, but then I thought my life was over. The *why* is not important anymore. Carl was pissed when he found out. Liam had already started tattooing on inanimate things. He loved to draw and discovered tattoos from some history documentary. Carl pushed him to do this. After, is when Liam and I figured out what we could do with it. We decided then it would be our secret. Obviously, they have figured out that something related to the tattoos has made a connection between us. Carl hates that he still doesn't understand more."

"Kate wants you to keep them covered." I say to him.

"If she would have been home that day, I don't think she would have let it happen. It was not long before Liam started coming to me talking about the '*itch*' to do it again. They separated us for a while. Of course, that did not stop our communication, but they didn't know that." He pauses in thought. "I think the first one and the ones that started on my face were the ones she wanted hidden most. It did not hurt me to cover them up and she was easier to get along with when they were covered. It just became what I did." He pauses again. He looks at me and a happy feeling ripples the air. "Then you came along and looked at me. Probably the first person who didn't flinch away at the sight of me." He moves to stand between my legs that are dangling from the countertop. I lean into him and kiss him. I hold him to me until he finally whispers in my ear, "We should get downstairs."

"I have so many more questions. Do we have to?" I whine playfully.

He smiles. Kisses me again. "If we don't go, they will just come for us." He reasons.

I pull him to me and kiss him deeper. I do not want this to end. I do not want to face whatever is waiting for us outside this room. I am completely head over heels falling for him. Out there the reality of what is happening scares me. He gently pushes me back and pulls me off the counter.

Reluctantly, I follow him down to join the others at breakfast. The table is filled with all the same people. I look at them each wondering who has what kind of abilities. Do they all have some kind of gift or power? I examine their eyes. Looking for who could be a threat and who could be an ally.

Fourteen

After breakfast, Felicia pulls me to the side. "Come with me." Lane nods for me to follow her. She walks quickly through the halls. I follow at her heals. "Things will move quickly now. Talk is going around that that boy has finally come into his power. The teetering of power will start leaning now."

"The teetering of what power?"

"Discussions have been in the works for a long time. A truth, kept secret, will be revealed soon. All hell's going to break lose." She opens a door. Inside is an entertainment room of some sort. Oversized sofas scatter between pool tables and other types of games. A dart board on the wall. A large TV screen nearly covers the wall at the end of the room. "I am calling all the young ones to meet in here. Us old folk are having a meeting of our own. You all should have an opinion."

"Felicia, I am not that young." I argue like a stubborn child. Then I think, maybe I am young. If I am so offended to be called young.

"You are the youngest of them all." She glares at me. "That boy, he has to be coming up on ninety."

A small laugh escapes my throat. I suck it back

when her glare intensifies. "There is no way he is ninety. Supay may be ninety, but not Lane."

"Supay." She thinks for a moment. "If I remember right, he is about in his late two-hundreds."

Liam enters the room then. "Felicia, I let everyone know to meet here. Now what?"

"Good, good." She pats his shoulder as she leaves the room.

He turns to me, "What are we supposed to be doing?"

"She says that all hell is about to break lose and that us young folk should have an opinion." I shrug. "Does that mean anything to you?"

"She has to be talking about picking which of the three outcomes we talked about earlier." He says as he moves to a counter space. The cabinets are filled with snacks and a small refrigerator is fully stocked with drinks in bottles and cans.

Others start to fill in. Setting up in small cliques throughout the room. Tina and Tracy are here too. Lane is the last one to finally walk in the room.

Lane starts the strange gathering of a meeting. "The elders want us to make opinions about how we feel. Choose sides. I don't think that is what we should be concerned with." The mood in the room shifts. My tattoo tingles with a chill. I find Liam's face. He is scolding me. I shrug at him and try to ignore the emotions in the air for his sake. He winks at me and my tattoo tingles again. "I think it is more important that we train." Lane continues.

Tina speaks first, "I don't have any powers to train with."

The attitude in her voice pulls my nose in a sneer. My tattoo spikes with cold. More painful than any other time. I glare at Liam. He raises an eyebrow at me.

"Having powers isn't the only thing we need to be ready for. Felicia and Dean do not have powers. They are still necessary in the minds of the elders." Liam counters.

"Dean is an intellect. He knows Him firsthand. He holds value there. Felicia is wise and may not have powers but is close with her beliefs in the spiritual world." A man, I recognize from the dining room and hallways, but I do not know his name, explains.

"Ok, ok I will start." A lively girl says bouncing in her seat. "My name is Lizzie. This is my sister Beth." She points to the girl sitting next to her. She smiles shyly. "We have an affinity for plants. We can make anything grow." She finishes with a giggle.

We are not seated exactly in a circle, but we continue around the room. With a heavy sigh the man who spoke says, "Hi. I am Kyle. I wield fire."

Next to him. "I'm Dave. I can turn my skin to stone." The skin across his arm ripples and changes from smooth, healthy, looking skin to a dry, deeply pored, stone. He taps it against the table next to him for effect. Thump, thump, thump.

Tina goes next, "I'm Tina. I can make a mean daiquiri." The room laughs. That is Tina, always the life of the party. I look away from her.

Lane says, "Don't worry, I am sure daiquiris will come in handy."

"I'm Tracy. I was once the caretaker of the fallen angel." Her voice is filled with animosity. She does not look at me and the room fills with whispers.

Luke clears his throat. "I am Luke. I can manipulate water." He pulls the attention of the room back to the mission at hand. Get to know everyone.

"I am Liam. I do tattoos." He shares a look with Lane.

"Lane." He points to his chest. "I've recently learned that maybe I can make ice. That is why training is important to me."

"I am Sara. I can read minds and sometimes I can persuade people to make certain decisions. I don't use it often." She adds.

Carl said that she was the one who warned them that I would explode. Could she have been in my mind at some point?

"Miley. I can turn into a wolf." She claims proudly.

"A dog, you mean." Kyle teases.

"It's really more like a bear. Its bigger than any kind of dog or wolf I have seen." Sara says in Miley's defense.

The banter settles and every set of eyes looks at me expectantly. "Jane. Fire." I say suddenly feeling very self-conscious.

"Just say it. You are the fallen angel." Tracy spits across the room.

"We don't know that for sure. I sure don't feel like I'm something so important." I retort.

"Let's just work with what we know is true for now. Kate and Carl have not used their powers in years. Kate is a charmer. Carl has strength and speed. They choose life over their powers though. Much like Pacha and Supay. As we age, using our powers can take years from our life span." Lane explains.

"I've never seen them used but I believe Pacha's powers have something to do with the sun and moon." Sara says.

"Supay is known as a death master, but I also don't know what that means in practice." Kyle adds. "Brock, my father, has the ability to control electrical currents."

"Edna isn't much to look at now, but she was once a strong warrior. It is believed that she is Amazonian." Lane says. She seems so small and weak now. It is hard for me to imagine her as a female warrior.

"Do any of you know any others?" Liam asks the room.

"The small town near here has a haven for outcasts. They mostly disguise themselves. Our small town is welcoming to them. We do not bother them unless they do something illegal. I can't say how many have powers though." Lizzie answers.

"That is great, a whole town of cowards." Kyle barks.

"I think this training should be free of judgment." Lizzie says sweetly.

At the same time Luke says under his breath, "The apple doesn't fall far from the tree on that one."

"You got something to say water boy?" Kyle tries to provoke Luke. Their emotions spike.

Liam freezes my tattoo. I look at him pointedly. The emotions grow. The air begins to ripple. Liam stands coughing once. "All right, it won't help anything if we fight amongst ourselves. Let's just agree to help each other train. I think the two of you should go head-to-head. Just not in my game room."

"I'd pay to see that." Miley laughs.

The mood lightens. Liam plops back in his seat. My cheek tingles. "I think that is enough talk. Let's meet in the back yard to start training after dinner." Lane announces. Everyone exits the room in a trickle.

Liam stops Lane before we leave. "Are you sure?" He asks.

Frustrated that they hardly talk aloud to one another. "Sure, of what?" I ask.

"Liam doesn't agree that we should train with them." Lane answers.

Liam's eyes go wide. "Did neither of you see how quick things got heated just now?"

"It is the only plan we have right now." Lane responds as he guides me out of the room.

From behind us Liam argues, "So, this is it, we start training with the possible enemy?"

"They can't all be our enemies." I retort. "If the

elders are not going to tell us what they know, then we can't blame anyone for how they choose to side."

Liam is better at controlling his emotions than anyone else. I can barely feel his frustration brewing. "Because the elders won't tell us what they know, we have to be careful who we trust." He retorts.

Lane is on the other side of this debate. "Trusting them isn't the same as training with them." He insists.

Fifteen

Lane and I make our way to the dining room. Both lost in our own thoughts, we walk in silence. Kate calls out from behind us. "Lane. Can I see you for a minute?" He looks at me, then to her. "Just you, please."

"I will be fine." I lean up to kiss him. He squeezes my arm before walking back to where she waits. I continue to the dining room.

I do not make it far when I cross paths with Carl. "Well, hello there." He greets me.

"Hi." I try to keep walking. He reaches out to grab my arm. I snatch away and take two steps away from him.

"I hear you have given Lane his power." He says pointedly.

"I didn't give him anything." I retort.

"Mighty convenient. You show up and now he walks around wearing his own skin with pride and shooting ice from his body. The prophecies are coming true." He says to me. I resent that what he says does add up with some of their beliefs. I will myself not to believe it. "Too bad he won't live long enough to see his true potential."

"Are you threatening to kill your own son?" I ask in

astonishment.

"He is not my son." He growls. He straightens his back finding his composure. He clears his throat as if he is going to say more. He decides against it and walks away. A strange emotion trails him. *Regret* maybe.

I continue to the dining room once more. I do not have time to think about what Carl said to me. Waiting at the bottom of the stairs is one of the older men, either Dean or Brock, I am unsure of which is which, he stops me.

"Jane. Quickly, come with me." He waves his hand for me to follow him to the throne room. The name I have decided to call this room. "Come now, I don't have much time to waste."

Hesitantly, I follow him. Inside, he ducks to a dark corner. Still motioning for me to follow. I can feel the urgency pulsing around him. I get close enough to him that he grabs my arm and pulls me within inches of him.

"His name. It is Moloch." His eyes dart around the room. "He will come for you and his son." I think he reads the confusion on my face. "Listen to me. You are the fallen angel. Though it is not quite the whole truth of the story. When you go back you must take Him with you. That is the only way things will be set right." His head jerks. He scans the room again. Then he takes a deep breath through his nose. "Oh no, this will make things even more difficult." I look around the room too. "I am afraid you won't have time to let it come to culmination. It saddens me to tell you this." He looks down at his hands.

A sadness blows through the air around me. I try

to avoid it for Liam's sake, but I cannot. My cheek freezes. I try to think, *I am fine. Please do not come for me.* I do not know if he will understand.

"No!" Dean shouts. "You can't tell anyone. Not him. Nor the father of your young." His eyes dart around the room again. "I must go. You must find a way to leave and take Him with you. It is the only way. You must take back your gifts. You must bring the balance back between our worlds." He takes my hand in his and kisses the back of my knuckles. He ducks farther into the shadows and I lose sight of him.

Liam slams through the door. "What is happening?" He demands. His eyes search the room for a threat. I look around the room too. I do not see Dean anywhere. Liam crosses the short distance to me. "You can't tell me not to come for you. I will anyway." He says seriously.

"So, you can read my thoughts."

"It is not always clear. When you are specifically talking to me though, it is loud and clear." He answers. His body still tense.

"Do you know what I know?" I think in my head, *answer through the tattoo but say 'no.'*

"No. It doesn't work like that." A trail of chill bumps follows the line of the tattoo on my face. I think in my head, *do not tell Lane.*

His lips purse. He looks away from me as he has some internal debate with himself. Aloud I beg, "Please, Liam."

"Come on, Lane knows I was coming for you." He

places a hand high on my back and guides me back into the hall. He starts to say something once the door closes behind us. I stop him and think, *Not here.*

Lane is running down the hall toward me. He scoops me up in his arms. "What happened?" He demands. He puts me down and looks at me all over.

"I am fine."

"Lane, we should find somewhere to talk." Liam says. I look at him with daggers in my eyes.

"We don't know who we can trust here." I say under my breath.

The tap of Kate's shoes against the wood floors announces her approach. "Lane, I wasn't finished talking to you." She looks each of us over. "Something wrong?" She asks.

I answer. "No, we are fine."

"Then I will finish what I was saying." She looks pointedly at Lane. "Liam, Lane, and Luke will be taking a short trip. You both need to pack an overnight bag with enough for two days. Jane you will stay here with Felicia and the others. You are welcome to everything we have here. Make yourself at home."

As she talks, a strange ripple of emotion moves from her towards us. Not an emotion she if feeling. An emotion she is pushing. This must be what a charmer means. She is trying to keep our reactions to this news calm.

Liam smiles. "Sure. What time should we be ready to go?"

"One hour." She turns on her heel and walks away. I stare watching her leave.

"I'm not going." Lane announces after she is gone.

"Is that spot safe? The one from before." I ask.

Sixteen

Liam leads us back to what is a tiny garden surrounded by hedges. It is beautiful here in the daylight. Liam and Lane both takes seats. I pace the grassy area in front of the fountain. "I can't tell you everything I know. I don't know how much you already know, Liam." I say to him.

"You can't hold this all into yourself." Liam says.

Frustration and jealousy surround Lane. "I am missing something. Why aren't you telling me what is going on?"

"I asked him not to." I admit. "I was given some information with orders not to tell anyone. Liam... well you know. I'm trying to hold back information from him too, but I don't know exactly how to do that."

"You can tell me here." Lane gestures around us.

Holding my promise to Dean, a promise I did not exactly make, I change the subject. "Kate is using her powers." I blurt. They both look at me like a horn is growing out of my head. "Neither of you thought it was strange that she asked you to leave for two days and you both said, 'yeah, sure whatever you say,' until she walked away." They both think it over. "Carl said something strange to me earlier."

"What?" Liam asks.

"He said you weren't his son." I say to Lane. The two of them share a look. "What?" It is starting to annoy me when I know they are talking through their connection.

Lane stands and takes my hands in his. "We are going to go with Kate. You stay here and train with the others. Only use fire. Do not tell them anything you know. Decide who you can trust."

This is not the direction I was hoping for. "What about Carl?"

"We will convince Kate to take him with us." Liam answers.

Lane pulls me in for a hug. He whispers in my ear, "Liam will be able to hear you no matter how far we go."

We do not say anything else. Without speaking it, we all know that it is probably not safe to talk on the property. We worry that we have already said too much. I try my hardest not to think about the things Dean said to me. Mostly so I do not expose Liam to too much. Also, we do not know for sure what Sara's mind control means. She could have access to our minds, and we may not even know it. I help Lane pack in silence. I can feel that it is not easy for him to leave me here. He does not like that we cannot discuss the information we are each holding back.

He holds on to me for a long time when it is time that they must leave. I force myself to let him go. I wave them off from the front porch. Kate never said more about where she was taking them. They all pile in one SUV. Kate driving and Carl in the passenger seat. The guys in the back. I cannot see them once they close the doors. The dark tint on the windows blocks my view. As they disappear down the drive, the emotions they carried with them go away too. An emptiness settles inside me. I did not realize how much I relied on those emotions to keep me connected to him. I did not even realize that I had them until recently. I wonder, for a moment, if I would have felt this empty even if I did not realize what I was feeling. *Yes.* I answer myself.

Back inside, I start the search for the others. I run into Felicia first. "You seem to be on a mission child." She says to me with a sideways glance.

A speech I have practiced in my head recites out of my mouth. "I think it is important that we prepare. Those with powers should be training. Those without could be helping gather as much information as possible." Hopefully, it does not sound suspicious and shows urgency.

She makes an *'umhm'* sound as she walks away. This is not odd behavior for her, but I cannot help but worry that she just seen right through me.

I take a deep breath when I find Tracy sitting in the tearoom alone. I take a seat on a sofa opposite her. "Hi." She looks at me over a cup of tea. "I would like to ask for your help." She puts her cup down and leans back in her seat. I feel her resistance already. I choose my words carefully. "Those with powers need to start training. They need to learn to control them. We need someone to find out what we are up against."

"What about the ones who think taking you down

is the way we all survive?" She says with a grin on her face.

"If that is the case then we will take that path. We still need someone to make sure that will work."

"You would die for these people, people you barely know, in order for them to survive." She gives me a look like she does not believe me.

"Look, it's obvious I don't believe that is the case, but if it came down to my life or all these people, then I would do the right thing. One life isn't more important than hundreds, or even more." I feel the truth in my words. It is hard to swallow that it could be a real outcome. I push the thought of Dean's conversation away as it tries to pass through my memory.

"What do you expect me to do?"

"We need to find these prophecies. Decipher them ourselves. We also need to understand the different outcomes that everyone believes."

"So, what, you try to find a happy medium? A politically correct answer? Bring all the world together in peace. Ha!" Sarcasm blankets her rhetorical questions.

"If anyone can do it, it's you." I put the ball in her court. She knows, as well as I do, that the only other person I could give this job to, out of our small selection, is Tina.

She sits in thought for what feels like an eternity. "Fine. I will see what I can find out." She picks up her cup. "I will need Tina."

"She's yours. Anything else that you need, that is at

our disposal, is yours too."

Before I can walk away, she says, "You know I have been working with Carl since I met you. He says I will be gifted powers when this is all finished. As long as I continue to make sure he has access to you."

I do not meet her eyes. I do not lash out at her like my heart wants me to. Instead, I say, "I am hoping that your closeness with them will help you attain the information we need." I pause before adding, "I hope things work out in your favor." I walk out of the room.

Seventeen

Tracy and Tina have gone somewhere in the manor with the intentions of research. Tina said she had been in the library before. We are all hopeful they find the prophecy that is spoken of so often. The rest of us gather outside in the far back corner of the property. The wall of fence stretches along two sides. The manor looks small, far off in the distance. A wooded area lines the back of the property. I assume it is surround by more of the fence somewhere deep inside. Here in the center of all that is a large opening. A small pond sits nestled in the corner of where the stone wall meets the tree line. We placed a few buckets near it in case a fire needs to be put out.

Sara and Beth have already set up a blanket to sit on. Beth is allowing Sara to explore her mind control abilities with the promise of not causing anything dangerous on purpose. They both look deep in thought. Lizzie kneels near the pond. Flowers bloom and wilt under her hands that flutter in the air above them. Dave brought a few boards, bricks, and odd shaped stones to practice… *smashing*. He turns his arm to stone and brings it down hard on a board stacked on top of two bricks. The wood splinters down the middle with the contact. He moves that piece and pulls forward another one. Miley is running through the wooded area in her wolf shape. She went in before she shifted and has not returned since. I am curious to see what she looks like as a wolf. Kyle is the only one who seems uninterested in training. He leans against a tree just outside of the shadows cast from the woods. He is ripping the leaves and twigs from a branch he found.

I decide to talk to him. "Hi, Brock." He does not look up. "You can manipulate fire, right?" No response. "I was, eh, wondering if you'd like to spar."

Hmph. "Sorry little girl. I wouldn't want to hurt you." He says without looking up.

I maintain my composure. "Do you not think it's important for us to learn our limits?"

"My father has been training me since birth. I will be ready for whatever comes." He finally looks at me. I regret wishing he would, seconds ago. "My clan believes you have to die for us to survive. You are the threat that brings Him here. You should be more concerned with hiding rather than training. If He does not take you out, one of us will for Him."

"Keep your friends close and your enemies closer." I repeat to him one of the sayings Felicia had told me growing up.

"Looks to me like you are short on friends." His face pulls to a sneer.

I feel his heat rising in the air around us. He does not make a move to attack. When I turn my back though, he will. I know it. I do not know how I know. It is not like I can hear his thoughts or see the future. I just know that when I turn around, he will throw his heat at me.

Not knowing exactly what that will look like I turn my back. His heat flares up, the air heating up all around me. I hear the flames growing as he manipulates them. I feel it building and then hear the release. I turn around with both hands out in front of me. I catch a ball of flames between my hands. Bigger than a basketball. Almost as big as a beach ball. I hold it, move it around in my hands, the color is different than I expected.

I look across the space at him. Over his own flames that I hold. "Blue? Have you always created blue flames, or have you learned to make it this hot?" I ask him. Genuinely curious. Also, trying to cover the shock of what I just did. *I caught a ball of flames. In my bare hands. Do not let him see that you do not know what you are doing.* I tell myself.

His eyebrows come down and together over his eyes. His chin dips down. His eyes do not leave me. He looks like a bull about to charge a matador. I focus back on the ball of flame in my hand. I cannot just throw it aside, but I need my hands free. I think about making the ball smaller. To my surprise, and Kyle's, it does what I want. The ball gets smaller. I do not know if he can tell, but my hands absorb the heat and flame coming from it. I feel it enter my body and fill me with its power. It becomes a part of me. The ball of flame disappears. My attention goes back to Kyle who is now running at me. I put my hands up, unsure of what to do next.

A loud sound of body against body. Two separate breaths are blown out around deep grunts. In front of me Dave has tackled Kyle. They both stand and face off against each other.

Dave barks out at Kyle, "He said to wait until He arrives."

Kyle's body relaxes. "I wasn't going to kill her." He adjusts his shirt. "Screw this. I'm not helping her train." He storms off back to the manor.

A large wolf emerges from the woods. She sits panting. She does look more like a bear than a wolf if you only consider her size. Her face though, is more menacing than a bear or wolf. Like she could be rabid. Her eye teeth are so long they hang past her jaw like a saber tooth tiger. A yawn stretches her jaws wide apart, revealing that all her teeth are just as dangerous looking even if they are shorter. She licks her lips and lies on the ground.

Dave follows my gaze to look at Miley too. "We aren't what you expected are we?"

"You are more than I expected." I answer honestly. "She's beautiful and intense."

Miley's ears go back in defense. "She knows what she is." Says Dave.

"Does she? Do any of you?" I ask them. "This is amazing. Maybe it is because I am just learning about it all, but these things we can do, they are incredible. I worry we are being used for something none of us understand, for an outcome that may not be in the favor of all of us."

My words must have carried to everyone in the clearing. I feel the entire air around me shift. I look around to everyone. They are all watching me. Miley's ears are positioned comfortably atop her head. Chill bumps follow the lines of my tattoo. Liam must feel that

I may have just gotten through to them even if it is just a small bit.

"You are probably right." Dave says. He drops his head. "If the others look like they are winning, I will walk with them." He admits. I can feel his shame.

"I understand the will of survival. I will not judge you, or any of you, if that is a choice you must make. All I ask is that until that time, let us be open minded to other options." I say to all of them.

Lizzie crosses the clearing to stand beside me. "I would like to give you something." She tells me. "Stand back."

I do as she says. We all watch as she kneels to the ground. She hovers her hands over a bare spot on the earth. A small bud pops out of the ground. Two small leaves bloom and spread. The skinny trunk starts to widen as it grows taller, more leaves bloom as it begins to send branches out from all sides. It grows taller than me in seconds. Its trunk begins to twist like a rope twisted out of nylon. Only it has grown so thick I do not think I could wrap my arms around it. The branches get heavier as more leaves sprout up and down them. They bend and wave in the wind. Minutes later, a weeping willow tree stands above us. Her branches hanging down and around like an umbrella. The ends sweeping the grass. I look at Lizzie as she looks up at the giant tree she created. Dave is the only other person who was close enough to be under it with us. He too is admiring the high branches and twisting trunk.

Lizzie starts talking. "She is grown from the spirits of the earth. She is your very own safe place. She can only offer you privacy and limited protection. She cannot attack or cause harm. She is not invincible."

"She, is a tree." I say aloud.

"Yes, she is." Lizzie announces proudly. "She is of the earth. The earth's power is the most important power there is. The earth and her balance with the moon and sun and all the universes."

I am not sure I understand what she is talking about, but I appreciate her enthusiasm. Her passion. We invite everyone under to see what Lizzie has built. Miley stays in her wolf form as she walks under the branches of the tree. She sniffs around before finding a soft spot to lie down.

An easy silence falls over the group under the willow. Each person lost in their own thoughts. "I am not going to rush you all off, but I think we have done enough training today."

I hate to break the silence. I do not want anyone feeling obligated to sit here. I want them to make their own choice. No one leaves. I quietly approach Lizzie. She has been growing simple bushes at the trunk base of the willow.

"Thank you so much for this." I gesture to the trunk of the tree.

"I am going to allow these to bloom on their own." She points at the last little bush she has started. "You will see. All will work out." She smiles at me.

She stands back and admires her work. I watch her as she walks away. The leaves and branches of the willow separate like curtains lifting on a stage. On their own. I am caught in a moment of awe at the impressive power that Lizzie holds. Followed by a sadness, *such a beautiful gift should never be used in combat.*

Dave ducks out of the branches. He has to physically move them out of the way. He comes back after a moment with a neatly folded stack of clothes. A pair of shoes hangs from his fingers. He places them on the ground behind the trunk. Miley stretches as she stands. Then lazily walks around the trunk. I hear her shift, more so, I feel the power of her shift. When she comes back around the trunk, she is her human self again. Her lips lift in a soft smile at me, she follows Dave out. He holds the branches for her.

Beth comes to stand next to me. She places a hand on my shoulder and smiles. Then she too leaves. Sara picks at her fingernails looking down at the ground. I walk over to her.

Before I can say anything, she blurts, "They will use me against you. I won't have a choice." She ducks out of the branches before I can stop her.

When I finally emerge from the branches the sun has gone down. The lights of the manor twinkle in the distance. I force myself to cross the darkened grounds.

Eighteen

Trying to sleep without Lane close by is harder than I imagined. I cannot seem to make my mind stop. I worry over how quickly I have become attached to him. I worry about what the future will look like. I play the conversation with Dean over and over in my head. He seems to believe I am the fallen angel. That I must leave and take Him with me. I push the thought of His name away. I do not know if Liam has already heard it through our connection. The elders are wrong for keeping all this secret.

I stop my mind from considering the other thing Dean mentioned. It is not possible. Or, if it were, it would be way too soon for him to know. Unless I made some decisions before when I was on the pills. I push the thoughts away with more intent this time.

All the paths ahead of me seem to point to an easy answer. The powers do not belong here. People are abusing them and using them to abuse others. If it really is up to me to restore balance, then that is what I will do. Not that I believe it.

The group at breakfast is the smallest I have seen. Only the people I trained with yesterday, Tina, and Tracy. Conversation picks up. Lizzie is excited about training again. We all agree to meet in the clearing again today. Kyle scowls at me. He leaves the dining room. I know he will not be there for training.

I catch up with Tracy in the hall as she heads to do more research. "Hey, I was just checking in. Have you found anything at all?" I ask. "No hurry. Just checking."

"No." She answers. "While I have you here, do you need a restock?" She asks through her teeth.

"No, thank you." I answer politely.

"Are you sure? The babysitters have all gone." She pushes. She pulls a hand from her pocket. She opens it slowly in front of me. Two pills roll in her palm.

"I am curious to what those things really are." I say to her. *I want them.* I push the yearning away. They most definitely will not help me.

"These are a product from the man himself." She tells me. "You made all of this very easy for being someone that is so important."

"You got them from Him?" I ask.

"Dean isn't the only one that knows him." She says proudly.

"Do you know him?" I ask.

"No, not directly." She answers. "Take them. You will feel better. I can only imagine how lonely you are without the love of your life by your side." She hisses.

"You have changed."

"You are so gullible. I have not changed. You are just seeing it now for what it always was." She pushes the hand with the pills closer to me.

    I take two steps back from her. Processing my own pain. She is right. Everything I looked at before I considered motherly. Now I see it. She had a mission to keep up with me. Keep me addicted to the pills. Wait for what comes next. I walk away.

    Lost in self-pity, I wander the halls. I reach out to Liam. For the third time today. No response. Something could be happening to them and I do not know how to use any of these powers to figure it out. Training seems like a waste of time. I will not be able to focus without knowing Liam and Lane are ok. I will not be able to focus even more because of the things Tracy said to me. She was never my friend.

    I find myself standing in front of the throne room. I am sure it has a proper name. Inside, all the chairs have been stacked to the side walls. The long table is pushed all the way to the back of the stage area. The row of thrones stands about where they have been every time I have been in this room. I walk down the row of thrones, admiring the intricate carvings on each one. I would not even know where to begin in figuring out their age or origin. They are beautiful.

    A shuffle, and a huff, has me jerking my body around to find the threat. In a heap, Edna is lying on the floor near a stack of chairs. I rush over to her.

    "Are you ok? Do I need to call for help?"

    I have to put my ear to her lips to hear her whisper, "Listen to the spirits. Don't die." I think is what she says to me.

Another sound has me looking back to where I was just standing. Carl stands just a few yards away from me. I try to pull Edna to standing. I feel the air around us change as Carl barrels toward us. I try to hurry and fail. He is there before I can blink. He holds Edna by the throat, her feet dangling in the air.

"Let her go. You want me. I am right here." I try to sound strong.

"I can't have you." He sneers.

A snapping sound and a release of breath drops me to my knees. I feel the anguish in my body before my mind finally catches up to what has just happened. He drops Edna's lifeless body to the floor.

I did not know her. I think the two sentences she spoke seconds ago were the first she has spoken in my presence. She just died because of me. Internally, I fight back against the emotions welling up inside me. Liam cannot help her now. No reason to upset him if he is able to hear me at all. *Wait, Carl was supposed to be with them. Maybe they are back.* I reach out slightly. No response.

"I wasn't expecting you to be in here. It is satisfying that you are." His lips lift in a half smile half sneer. "This is after all, because of you." He nudges her body with the toe of his boot.

The warmth of my anger travels slowly up my spine. The door opens and someone else enters the room. Brock stops once he is in full view of the scene in the floor.

His lips purse. "Carl, I thought you were on a trip with your family."

I did not know any of the elders were still here. No one else was in the dining room earlier. I have hardly noticed the cleaning staff. I watched Carl leave, yet he is back. Where has Brock been? Here the whole time?

"I cut my visit short. They are busy enough without me." Carl answers.

The tone of his voice puts me on high alert. Something is wrong. Very wrong.

"Killing Edna will turn out to be an unwise decision for you." Brock says.

"I did not kill her. She did." He shoves a finger in my direction. "Just as she killed Dean. You will find his body in the pool."

"Carl you were warned not to take matters into your own hands. We know who the resisters are. It is not our decision to start killing them." Brock says.

"I won't wait for Him any longer. He dumped his kid on my doorstep, I raised him, I have done everything He has asked of me and received nothing in return. Now this shows up and destroys my hard work. Turns my sons against me. I think I will kill her just to see what happens." He starts to move toward me.

The anger from him pushes me back. Physically pushes me inches away from where I stand. I cannot stop Liam from feeling that one. I am starting to worry that he cannot feel it.

Brock loses what little patience he had. "Carl! Where is Kate?" He is anxious about Carl's response.

Carl's anger turns to Brock. I search the back of the

room for an escape. I know the elders used doors back here to enter and exit.

Carl's emotions turn ravenous. Dangerous jealousy. "Brock, why does my wife's where abouts concern you so much?"

I spot a short staircase in the darkest corner of the room. I do not look back as I feel electricity in the air. The hair on my arms lifts. A deafening boom echoes. Something crashes behind me. I jump down the short set of stairs. I hit the door and it slams open. The sun blinds me for a second. I am outside. I take off running as fast as I can through the courtyard garden, past the pool. Where sure enough, a body floats face down. I do not stop as I continue running towards the willow tree.

The tattoo on my face freezes. The pain brings me to my knees hard. My body topples over itself before finally landing on my back. "Where are you?" I shout into the sky.

Suddenly I know. My frozen face does not let up. I see the direction ahead of me. It is invisible, like the air has a fold in it. A fold leading back around the front of the house. I jump back to my feet and without looking around I follow the fold.

On the other side of the house, the fold in the air leads down the driveway. I start running. At the end of the drive the fold veers off to the right. I continue running down the side of the road. The wall of the property is visible here. In my peripheral vision, I watch as it almost seems to run along with me. My frozen cheek somehow gets colder. The pain spikes. I cover it with my hand as I fight to maintain my balance against it.

The wall of the property suddenly ends but the fold in the air keeps me moving forward. I scold myself for not taking a car. Who knows how far away they are? A pain in my side awakens as I push my muscles to keep me up right and running. My body protests, when suddenly the fold has me taking a hard right. A hidden driveway. Two worn paths of tire tracks mark out the drive. I power through the pain in my side and ignore my screaming calf muscles. Ahead I see a small building. *He is there.*

The fold disappears and the air is normal again. I slam through the door at the front of the building. No one is inside. In a panic I start searching all the rooms in the place. There are not many. Empty. Broken pieces of furniture sit alone, covered in a thick layer of dust. I run back to the door where I entered. A strange sound from my footsteps against the floor has me skidding to a stop.

I stomp around until I hear it again. The floor is hollow. I find the handle under a lose board and lift a large square section up. A ladder leads down into the darkness. Crumpled at the bottom of that ladder is a large body. I quickly make my way down the ladder to him. His face is savagely beaten.

"Liam. Liam." I pull his face to look at me. His eyes flutter.

"Jane." His voice is barely over a whisper. It comes out raspy. "Lane." He points down a tunnel like hallway. There is no light other than from the open floorboards above our heads. "Go." He pushes up from the floor painfully. "I will be ok. Go."

Begrudgingly, I leave him there. Hopeful he will be there when I get back. I run into the darkness of the tunnel. With the fold in the air gone and no light to guide me, a panic starts to rise in my chest. I feel out for emotions or power in the air. Nothing. The tunnel curves sharply and opens to a large room. A single candle burns at the far end. I stop to ascertain my surroundings.

"Jane." A woman's voice barks at me. "You shouldn't be here." The tap of her heels, against stone, lead my senses in her direction. I still cannot see her. "This must mean Liam got free."

"Kate?" I ask into the darkness.

Nineteen

"You must understand that this was the only choice I had. Liam would not have gotten hurt if he would not have intervened. I suggest you turn back. Help him instead." Her heels stop tapping against the floor.

"Where is Lane?"

"His father is coming for him." She answers.

"Carl is back at the manor. Killing people." Does she not know what he is doing?

"Brock will take care of that. Who has he killed?"

"Edna and Dean." I answer.

I feel as she starts to use her power. In the dark I see a soft glow coming from her body. The air around her starts to ripple with the glow. If this were different circumstances it may be a beautiful sight. As it were, I use it to my advantage. I quietly move around the space to come up behind her. She does not seem to be able to see me. I keep my steps as soft as I can. I hesitate as I know what I am about to do. I put my hands together high above my head. I weave my fingers together and bring down the double fist, hard on the back of her head. Her glow goes out and she crumples to the floor. *She is not dead.* I tell myself. I leave her and move quickly toward the single candle at the back of the room. I find Lane in a heap on the floor.

"Lane." I whisper. I look back into the darkness. I do not know how long we have before she wakes up. "Lane." I nudge him. He jumps and moves away from me. "It's ok. It's me, Jane." I tell him.

"What… what are you doing here?" He struggles to stand. "You have to leave. He is coming."

"We have to leave. Come on." I try to pull him. He hesitates. "Lane, Liam is hurt too. We have to get out of here and find help."

He finally stands. He limps some as I help hold his weight with his arm over my shoulder. When we reach Liam, he is sitting up against the wall. Not alone. Luke is blocking the ladder. His arms crossed over his chest.

"Luke. They are hurt. I have to get them out of here." He looks down at Liam then up at Lane. "Please."

He snatches Liam from the floor by his shirt collar. Liam is dripping with water. "Who do you think hurt them?" Luke snarls.

Someone else moves behind Luke. "I told you," Sara says as she steps into the light, "they would use me against you."

I look at her then at Luke. This power, it scares me the most. She can turn my friends into my enemies. Make them do things to the people they love.

"What does someone have on you that would make you do this?" I ask her.

Lane yells out and drops to the floor. I try to help him. I look up and see that she is holding her hand out at us. Panicked I try to talk her down from this. "You have a choice. There is always a choice. You don't have to do this."

"You know nothing about me. You and your dreams of a happy fucking ending. Wake up! That is not the real world. Normal people do not accept our kind. They never will. I had to choose a side. One promises life, the other condemns me to life in a prison. A prison of my own mind. Never allowed to be who I am. I chose to be me. With the people who praise my power. You, you are a hypocrite. I can see into your mind. You would not allow me to run free with my powers. You would lock me away too." She ends her tangent waiting for my response.

I do not have one. Seeing her power in action, she is right, if it comes down to my choice for her, I will lock her away. This seems so wrong. This intrusion into other people's minds. Seeing Luke's body holding his nearly drowned brother at no fault of his own. This time I see her power. When she draws it to herself, she takes it completely away from Liam and Lane, leaving only a little to hold onto Luke's mind. I focus on her power and try to remember what I did with Kyle. I was expecting fire with him. It was a kind of fire, it was different from mine, and I was able to catch it. That is the only possibility I see ahead of me now. Catch it. Take it away.

I feel her power. I watch as it shifts the air around us. I see the faint glow of it. She pushes it away from her body. I put my hands up and will myself to catch it. It hits my palms hard pushing me back. I nearly trip backwards. I hold on to her power. She realizes what I have done and tries to pull it back to herself. I do as I did before and will it to get smaller. I crush it between my hands.

"No!" She cries out.

The power between us turns into a thin piece of thread as we each pull in a tug of war. Liam falls to the floor. Luke grabs on to his head with both hands. He sees us struggling. He punches her in the jaw. Her head snaps back. The last of her power whips toward me. I inhale deeply, and just like that, the struggle is done.

"Jane, I…," Luke starts to explain or apologize.

"I know." I say to him. "We have to get them out of here."

"I was there, but I wasn't there…" He tries again.

"Luke, you don't have to explain it to me. I know. Help me." I try to keep him focused.

Dust falls from overhead and footsteps echo on the wood floor above us. I panic. Taking Sara's power makes me feel full. I do not know if I can handle more right now.

"Jane? Jane, are you down there?" Lizzie's voice echoes down to us.

Luke looks up the ladder. "We are going to need some muscle help." He calls up.

"I'm coming down." Dave's voice, then his boots come down the ladder.

He and Luke discuss quickly how to get Liam and Lane up the ladder. They figure it out and start moving. Luke carries Liam who is starting to come to enough to help. Dave carries Lane with ease across his shoulder. I start for the ladder. I stop to gather my strength. Sara's body crumpled beside me. *I cannot leave her.* I struggle to get her positioned on my shoulders the way Lane was on Dave's. Clearly, he is stronger than me. I teeter up the rungs of the ladder. My hand grabs the last one when someone finally pulls the weight of her from me.

When I pull myself from the hole, everyone else is waiting. Sara is already tied down crudely to Miley's back, who is in wolf form. Dave has Lane across his shoulders and Liam leans heavily against Luke. Lizzie loops her arm through mine and we quickly follow everyone out the door.

We cut across the property into the woods. I am confused, but I trust this group and follow them in. With the extra weight of the wounded, we move slowly through the trees. We come to a service gate with a gravel path leading away to the road. Inside the gate, we pass through more woods before finally coming to the clearing with the willow. We all gather under the umbrella-like cover of her branches.

"Why are we here? Shouldn't we go to a hospital?" I ask.

Lizzie pats my arm as she moves to Liam. "We don't need a hospital."

Dave starts arranging Lane comfortably on the ground. Luke fills my vision. "Why did you bring her here?" He growls at me. Pointing at Sara's body.

"We have bigger issues." Dave says to him.

Lizzie kneels first by Liam. Beth sits next to her. Liam watches her as she puts one hand on his chest and holds Beth's hand with the other. The power ripples through the air. The branches of the willow sway. Liam flinches and then relaxes. Quickly, she and Beth move over to Lane. She repeats the same motions. Lane does not wake up right away, but his breathing takes on a calm, normal pace. They move to Sara next. Luke starts to protest before Dave shoots him a look.

I sit on my knees next to Lane. I take his hand in mine. "He will wake soon." Lizzie whispers to me. The lines in my tattoo tingle. I look at Liam. He nods at me once. Lane squeezes my hand.

His eyes flutter open and I kiss him on the mouth. I jerk back realizing that maybe that was a little too aggressive. His hands take my face and pull me back to him. He kisses me.

Luke clears his throat. "Can we talk about this yet?"

"Where are we?" Lane asks.

"This is our safe space." Lizzie answers.

Luke's body shakes with his frustration. "Who the hell cares where we are?"

Sara, who is already sat away from the group, shrinks back farther. I stand and say, "We needed a safe place. Lizzie made this." I gesture to the tree.

"We can't trust these people. She was in my head. She is with them!" Luke fumes.

"We saved your asses back there." Dave counters.

Miley, still in wolf form, paces the back of the group. Sara is one of them. They will not let Luke run her out. I will not let Luke run her out. She warned me that she would do this.

"None of us can trust each other." I announce. "It is not possible. We do not know what or who we are against or what we are for. There are too many unknown factors at play here. No matter which side you think you are on." I explain.

Sara stands. "Tracy found information. She took it to Kate."

"I can't do this. I cannot stand here and let her speak among us. She is the enemy." Luke yells.

My own frustration gets the better of me. "Luke, I took her power. She stays." I decide.

Everyone goes silent. I know what this information means for them. Sara breaks down in sobs. Lizzie and Beth coddle each other. Liam looks down at the ground. Dave scowls at me. Luke's mouth hangs open in shock. Miley bares her wolf teeth at me. Lane stands to join my side. Every unanswered question about what has happened is forgotten. How had I found them? How had they found us? How Sara was there when I thought she was with the group training? None of that matters next to the threat of what I just made reality to each one of them. On my side or not. The silence is thick.

I can take the powers away. This revelation changes how each one of them will continue from here out. It answers at least one question that even the elders may have been asking. This confirms what Dean said. Some of these powers are beautiful and could be helpful, but they do not belong here. A small breach opens in my mind. Fragments of memories pass through.

    Dave gives words to the fear before I can process the images in my mind. "It is all true then. You are here to take the powers away."

Twenty

"I had to stop her. She was hurting Lane. She was using Luke's brain to hurt his brothers." I drop my head. "I didn't know that I could, until I started doing it."

I doubt any of them believe me. Lane wraps an arm around my shoulders. Liam looks at me meaningfully. It is time to tell them what I know. Allies or foe. The lines on my cheek tingle. I square my shoulders. All their eyes follow my every move. Most of them in distrust.

"His name is Moloch. He is one of the fallen. He fathered a son while he has been here." I pause to look at Lane. "He left him in the care of Kate and Carl with promises of more power." I take a deep breath. "I am one of the fallen. I think most of this is my fault. The only way things can be set right is to bring back balance. Lizzie knows about the spiritual world. Felicia knows about the spiritual world. My presence here is what has crossed the physical world and spiritual world together. With a little of where I come from mixed in. I have seen some beautiful things come from this accident," I look at Miley, "I have also seen some horribly inhuman outcomes from it." I look at Sara. Talking to her, "I don't blame you. Your reaction was caused by abuse from others who did not understand and did not try to understand. You were put in positions to make tough decisions. None of us can say how we would react given the same choices." I turn my attention back to the group. "Edna and Dean are dead. More could be by now. I can't let more death happen because I am here." I decide not to mention the possible pregnancy or that all this ends with me leaving. If I cannot stay, I cannot have the child.

Liam recovers from the onslaught of information first. "What does this all mean?"

"I need your help to take him back." I answer.

"Wait, what?" Lane asks as what I have said sinks in. "Take him back where?"

"I wish I knew more. I don't know where." I do not meet his eyes. I cannot face that pain right now.

Dave looks at me suspiciously. "Do you expect us just to fall in line? Do what you say. You are here to take our powers away."

"No. I don't expect anything. You can make your own choices. I will not come after you or attack you. I will defend myself and protect the ones I love. For as long as I am here." I answer. "Taking away the powers, I think, is just part of taking Moloch away. Apart from the extra dangerous powers in the hands of the wrong people or control. While I am here, I cannot allow people to abuse these powers if I have the ability to stop it."

"I am staying." Lizzie stands up. Beth stands too. She nods at me.

"I think I am going to take the high road. I am not

choosing a side. I'm going to live my own life." Dave says. Miley sits at his feet.

"I am staying." Liam says to me.

"Me too." Lane says into my ear. He hugs me to his side.

"I am staying." Luke says on a huff.

Sara looks down at her hands. "I'll stay. If you will have me."

I smile at her. Luke rolls his eyes and shakes his head. Dave holds his hand out to me. "Thank you." I take his hand; his shake is firm. "Maybe our paths will cross again before you go." Miley loops around me. She nudges my arm with her head. They leave together.

The tension between the rest of us is thick in the air. There are not enough answers to the questions swirling in their heads. I do not have time to go into it anymore tonight. We must face whatever may be going on in the manor.

We slowly make our way in silence across the grounds. Inside, we find Carl detained. He is in the main hall tied to one of the big chairs from the throne room. His head hangs awkwardly down into his chest. Brock enters from the dining room. He pauses to look at all of us. He is carrying a heap of chains in his arms. Behind him Kyle comes from the dining room carrying cuffs. He snarls at us.

Brock gives him a look. "We are restraining Carl so he cannot hurt anyone else." He continues with his task. As he works, Kyle joins him. He continues talking, "Arrangements have been made for Edna and Dean. For now, they are in the convention hall." He points to the room I have been calling the 'throne room'. "Pacha has not left Edna's side. She only just stopped crying." He stands satisfied with his work. "Where is Dave and Miley?" He asks Lane.

"We haven't seen them recently." He lies.

"I thought you were all training together." Brock asks.

Lane lifts an eyebrow at him. "Well, actually Liam, Luke, and I have just returned." He tells the truth. Part of it.

"Where is Kate?" Brock's voice takes on a different tone. Concern.

"She was with Carl, last time I seen her." Lane lies. Or maybe that is his truth. He was unconscious when I found him.

"Sara." Brock barks. "Where is Kate?" Sara flinches and looks at the floor. He starts to move toward her. I step in front of him using my body to block her from him. "Sara." He says more calmly.

Sara's voice shakes as she responds. "I lost control of her." I look back at her in shock. *Was she in Kate's head?* "They tried to escape. I had to switch focus."

Brock has known all along where Carl had taken them. He may not know the details of what brought us here, but he knows more than he is putting on.

"Find her!" He orders.

She shrinks back again. "I can't." Tears fill her eyes.

Brock starts pacing the floor in front of us. "I seem to have a growing problem." He continues pacing. "I am short two bodies. My strongest weapon seems to be out of order. And someone let the boys out." He controls his emotions well. I focus on the air around him trying to judge his next move. "I seem to have underestimated you." He stops in front of me. "Tracy." He calls out.

She scurries in. She hands him a stack of papers and a leatherbound book. "This is everything I could find." She tells him. She bends at the waist in a quick bow.

He flips through the loose pages. "Even without this information, that you tried to get a hold of, you seem to have figured out enough on your own." He holds up the book. "This was written by your friend Dean. Did he tell you what was in it?" I do not respond. He passes the papers and book to Kyle. "Too bad it has all been lost in a fire."

Kyle holds the stack in his hands. I watch the air around him shift as he hands blaze blue. Engulfing the stack in his flame. When he releases the flame, he lets the ashes float to the floor.

"I really hope poor Dean was able to warn you."

"That is enough!" A shout comes from the top of the stairs. Felicia makes her way down. "These children have been through enough. What is coming for them will be far worse than anything you or Carl can serve."

"Felicia, how great it is for you to join us." He nods his head at Kyle. Kyle leaves the group to the dining room. "You have always known that this is part of the plan."

"The plan never involved the deaths of our council." She retorts.

Kyle comes back into the main hall. He leads Supay to our group. Felicia's face changes. An eerie shadow fills the room. Its point of origin seems to be Supay.

"See, if you all would have had an opportunity to read that ledger you would know that our friend here is God of Death. You may have reconsidered the vote for him on council." Brock's lips lift in a half smile.

The shadow wraps around Felicia's legs. It smokes around her body, weaving itself all around her. No one else seems to notice. Not even Felicia herself. Until she tries to step back.

"What is this?" She asks.

"Time to go." Supay answers her. He brings a finger to her forehead. The tip barely brushes her skin.

I am the only one who reacts to the cacophony of sounds that echo through the hall. Felicia's body falls to the floor. My body lurches forward. The sounds get louder and louder. My ears ring. Then silence. Everything in the room goes still. Felicia stands. Not Felicia, more of a transfer copy of her. Her features are a translucent mist. A ghost. She floats close to my face. Blocking me from seeing anything else. Her voice comes to me in a song like whisper. *Run.*

The mist-like Felicia turns and flies to the farthest end of the hall. I take off after her. I follow her through the doors that lead to the back yard. She puts distance between us. I push my legs to their max, trying not to lose sight of her. I do not realize my feet are pounding against the ground below me until they are not anymore. Instead, they are splashing and sinking into... mud.

My shoe catches on a stray root and I fall face first with a splash of mud and muck. The taste of salt fills my mouth. Marsh? I struggle through the mud to stand. I am in a swamp. Cypress trees stand tall around me. With bulging bases near the water and tall slender trunks holding them in the sky.

I decide to keep running in the direction I was already headed. The mud slows me down making it hard to lift my legs. I spot somewhat of a path through the trees and veer to follow it. The ground here is firmer, and I pick up speed again. The plant life around me changes. Bushes fill the path and wider trunked trees line the way. Soon I lose the path to the overgrowth. Felicia's last word on repeat in my mind. *Run.*

The ground gets firmer under my feet. I jump over places where the brush is too high to run through and hop over fallen logs. A couple of places are too high to jump and too thick to run through. I weave around them. Hoping that I am still on the right track. The plant life around me starts to change again. The paths get clearer. The trees seem to grow in straight lines. I risk a glance around. A pine tree forest surrounds me. Tall trees mirror each other down perfectly spaced rows. Pine needles cover the ground under my feet. I slip a few times but maintain my advancement forward.

A loud crack from above me has me covering my head with one arm. I do not waste the time to find the source. *Keep moving.* Another crack. Closer this time. I skid to a stop as one of the trees crashes down in front of me. A succession of cracking sounds fills the air around me. I hop over the tree blocking my path and slam my feet into the ground. Pushing off as hard as I can to move as fast as I can. I wobble as the ground under my feet begins to shift in time with the crashes of the falling trees behind me. The forest behind me sounds like it is caving in on itself. The trees ahead of me begin to sway back and forth. Lifting the earth that is burying their roots. Another tree falls in my path. I hop over it without slowing down. *Keep moving.* I will myself.

The ground under me seems to disappear. I fall. The momentum of my body slams into the ground. I shake off the confusion. I have landed in a shallow hole created by a tree ripping its roots from the dirt. I use the broken pieces of root sticking out to pull myself back to level ground. I survey the path ahead. The ground all around seems to be moving like the waves of the ocean. The trees that remain standing wheeze and sigh in the air. In unison the standing trees slam to the ground. I cover my face and kneel to the ground as branches and broken pieces of bark fly all around. The air goes silent. I cautiously move my arms.

The land all around me is flattened. A glint of light in the distance ahead of me captures my attention. Dodging holes dug out by tree roots and jumping downed trunks, I head towards the glint. Closing the distance, I start to make out a small cabin. A single trail of smoke billows toward the sky from a thin chimney. The front door stands open. The source of the glint of light is a broken window next to the doorway. I slow my pace as I search for threats. From outside I cannot see inside the small house. I dart to the outside wall of the door frame. Avoiding the window. I press my back against the house and peer around the corner through the open door.

A small fireplace sits directly from the door on the back wall. The embers left from a recent fire glow red hot inside the hearth. The ground from outside transitions through the threshold of the door and into the room. *Dirt floor poor.* Felicia always described her childhood this way.

"Hello?" I call into the darkness. "I saw the smoke from your chimney. I hate to impose, but I am lost." I wait for a response. "I'm going to come in." The sound of my voice bounces around the room.

I nervously step into the cabin. My eyes slowly adjust to the lack of light. The space is completely empty. Just the four walls and the fireplace. No other windows or doors anywhere. No furniture or decorations. A pot hangs above the embers on a hook in the fireplace. The darkness seems to swallow up the room around me. I take another step into the room. The door slams closed behind me making me jump and spin around. No one is there. I put my back against the door.

A sound comes from left side of the room. My heartbeat skips. I try to listen. A shuffle echoes off the wall from the right side of the room. I search the door, with my hands behind me, for the doorknob. Fear takes over me as I hear another sound from the left side of the room. I frantically spin around searching for any handle to open the door. I heat up trying to burn the door down.

"Useless here." A thick grumbling voice calls from the left side of the hearth. I freeze with fear.

"Protected." A slightly more feminine scratchy voice says from the right.

"I've waited." The first voice.

"A long time." The second.

They are finishing one another's sentences. I turn around to see who is there. I cannot make out anything in the dark. I ask the only thing I can manage to get out.

"Waited? For me?" Both corners send shuffling sounds toward me. As if they are moving forward. I position myself for an attack.

"You came to me." The first voice says from the left.

"The first that ever has." The second voice says from the right.

"Put me back." The left.

"I am broken." The right.

The shuffling seems so much closer, but I still cannot see them. I light a fire in my palm. Willing the flame to grow. The light struggles against the shadows. Finally, the light succeeds and about halfway across the room from me two, thin, sick looking female bodies stand. Both wearing rags for dresses with stringy black hair falling down their shoulders. Their faces sunken. Cheek bones jutting out and deep, sunken, eye sockets. They look identical to one another. Neither one flinches at the light I have created in the room.

"Who are you?" I ask.

"Broken." The left growls.

"Broken." The right wails out.

A new voice fills the room. Felicia says, "They are from your home. Whatever brought you here, spilled your world into ours. This is our spiritual realm. Their presence has destroyed this place of peace. You must send them back."

"Felicia, I don't understand. I don't know how to send them back." I answer into the emptiness around me. She starts to materialize.

"Only you and he know where you come from. Here we only know that something foreign has wreaked havoc on our lives. On our understandings of the world. Spirits from our own world have been set free and attached to human lives. Spirits or creatures from your world have taken up residences in our spiritual realm and our human realm. Balance is key to life here. I am sure it is key to your home too. I brought you here because these two are the darkest things I have been able to locate. My family has spent generations trying to find the spiritual anomalies. To correct the wrong. Then I found you. I failed you. I did not see the signs of evil that had woven its way through my trusted circle. That aside. I could not reach this realm in life. I understood that I only had one opportunity to get you here. I was too weak to do it sooner. Scared that it was the wrong path. Gods like Supay and Kay Pacha belong in my world's legends and mythology, not walking around us as powerful human beings. I hoped that you were sent here to do just that. I knew it was true when I watched you take a part of Kyle's gift. The others know it too. They do not want to give it up. They are addicted to the power. That is why they keep causing distractions. Slowing the inevitable." She goes quiet.

I look at the two rotting women. They are looking at me expectantly. They lift their right arms out toward me. Moving in perfect synch. A thought deep in my mind shifts. I cannot reach it. I lift my arm, holding my hand out to them. The air ripples at the center point of our outstretched fingers. The ripple grows and I know. I must take their hands. Her hand. I must guide her home. As our fingertips touch, three hands become two. The two women become one. A warm glow knits them together. A beautiful woman smiles down at me.

Her voice sings to me, "Finish. Come home." A light, blasts through the roof of the cabin. The woman floats with it. The light flicks away. She is gone. Felicia is gone. I collapse.

Twenty One

Something keeps tickling my face. I swipe it away and roll over. The crunch of grass beneath my head wakes me. I sit up. The branches of the willow sway away from me. I lean back against her trunk. Disoriented, I try to remember how I got here. The memories flood my brain. I grab my head with both hands. Too fast, too painful, the memories of Felicia dying, my chasing her, the swamp, and the woods, helping a broken spirit go home. The pain fades and I push up. I must finish. Finish what? I do not understand what happened or how I was able to do it. That place in the back of mind stirs. A memory that I cannot quite reach. The others are probably worried sick.

The branches of the willow part on their own as I walk from under her protection. I look back at her. She looks like a tree. A glorious, tall, tree. Nothing extraordinary. I now know that she is a gateway to the spiritual world. She led me to follow Felicia. She allowed me to cross the boundary between realms. She came from Lizzie, who can heal things just by touch, grow things with only a thought, and from whom I must take that power away. I turn back toward the manor.

My face freezes with the familiar touch of Liam's mind. I rush to find him. Before I make it halfway across the grounds, I see them filing out of the house. Lane first, followed by Liam, Sara, Lizzie, and Beth. Lane picks up speed running to me with all his might. I match his pace and we wrap each other together. Arms and legs, smiles, and kisses.

"We have been looking everywhere for you." He says, breathless.

"How long was I gone?"

"Two days." He answers.

"I couldn't find you." Liam says.

"We thought you left without saying goodbye." Lizzie says.

"We have a lot to discuss." I tell them all.

"We have plenty of time for that. Let us get you inside, fed, and cleaned up." Lane says. I look down at myself. Still covered in mud. My clothes dripping wet, like I just walked out of the swamp.

∞∞∞

At the dining table. Lizzie carries in a large tray of sandwiches. I have showered and changed. Lane has not left my side yet. The house is quiet except for us.

"What did I miss?"

Liam starts explaining. "When you ran off, Brock took Carl, Kyle, and Supay with him. We are not sure where. They took one of the cars from the garage. I think he even sent all the house staff home too. Tracy and Tina left without a word. Kate has not been seen. Brock arranged for Edna, Dean, and Felicia to be... taken away." He adds with a gulp.

Lane continues for him. "Pacha hasn't been seen since he took Edna away." He looks around the room at our group. "We all kind of fear that this is just a calm before the storm."

"Luke has locked himself away in his room." Liam adds.

"Probably because I am still here." Sara says.

"Where did you go?" Lane asks me.

I take a bite of a sandwich. I chew slowly. What I must tell them will be hard. Especially hard for Lane. I swallow and take a deep breath.

"I followed Felicia into the realm of spirits. I am from a different realm, or world, or time. I think, it is hard for me to understand because this mind is not from where I am from. I do not understand how we got here, but I know we must leave. Your powers come from spirits. Some from this world, some not. Both have to go back." All of them are looking back at me with confusion in their eyes. I hear the words that I am saying but I am not sure where they are coming from. Felicia hardly explained anything when I was with her; and yet, I seem to have so much information in my head. "The name Supay. Do any of you recognize that from anywhere other than the one we know?"

"Mythology." Sara says. "Brock told us that Supay is the God reborn."

"The god of what?" Liam asks.

"The God of Death." Sara answers. "I can't be sure, but I think our world has been breached many times before. Throughout all of history there are stories that don't make sense in the world we know and understand." Sara continues. "I loved mythology growing up. When Brock was training us, so many of his stories sounded like the ones in the history books. Only, he was talking about our present day. I could not control Supay's mind, but I could see it. His memories are old. Like really old." Abruptly she stops talking and looks at a place behind me.

Luke has entered the dining room. He takes a seat and grabs a sandwich off the tray. "Go ahead. Let the mind walker tell the stories of her adventures in other people's brains." He growls.

"Luke." Lane scolds.

"It is ok." Sara says. "I deserve it."

Beth speaks before anymore tension can build between Luke and the rest. "How long do we have? With our powers I mean." She speaks so rarely that it takes a moment for me to process.

"I don't have a good answer for that." I think for a while. "I will need your help to find Moloch. The powers are our only chance against him. There is a good chance he knows we are coming after him. I doubt he will go willingly." I pause. "Think of it like a jigsaw puzzle. I have the pieces of you all here. I have an idea of where you go, but before I can place you in your space, I have to finish the area around you."

Twenty Two

Lane has been silent since the dining room. We are finally alone in his bedroom. He is busying himself with putting away clothes in the large closet. I can feel his emotions pulsing through him. A swirl of frustration, sadness, anger, and fear. I sit at the foot of the bed and wait for him. He notices that I am waiting for him.

"You have to go." He tells me.

I answer, though he did not ask, "Yes."

"I can't make you stay." He admits.

"No," I answer, "but, it was your idea for me to make my own choices." I remind him.

He hangs the last shirt. Crosses through the dressing area and stands in front of me. "Can I influence those choices?" He asks as he leans his head to mine. His cool breath caressing my lips.

"Definitely." The fire in my belly lights. I pull him to me.

All the frustration that has built up in each of us, all the stress of saving the world, it all melts away in his arms. I feel his body relax from that and then tense with desire. He pushes me back on the bed. We snatch our clothes off throwing them to the floor. He mounts me and a wildness flashes through his blue eyes. The ice of him enters me. I meet his thrust with a moan. He hugs me to him, wrapping his arms around my body. I wrap my legs around his body and my arms around his neck. His mouth finds mine. Smothering a moan of his. His thrusts get harder, his size pushing on my walls as they stretch to accommodate him, my heat climbs. His ice consumes me. Every inch of me feels every inch of him. My body releases the tension and his is quick to follow. The ice shoots through me. Our heavy breathing slows as we bury ourselves in each other.

He rolls to sitting up. Taking me with him. Not pulling himself out of me. He puts his colds hands on either side of my face. He drags his fingertips down my neck. He cups both of my breasts. My body reacts to his touches and the fire lights again. Slowly I start rocking in his lap. His body reacts. He meets my movements. His hands slide down my sides then around to support my bottom. He guides my rocks to meet his thrusts. I feel my climax building again. He lays back watching my body as we move. The ice of him, only contacting my most sensitive spots, is a sensation like none I have felt before. My own heat rising and his ice at my center. I bounce harder as my body tenses. He holds me down against him. He releases first and my body rocks hard in reaction. A full moan fills the room. I am not sure if it is from me, or him, or both of us. Suddenly I am weak and fall to a heap on his chest. He wraps his arms around me. Holding me close. Cooling me down.

"I suppose this is what I get for falling in love with an angel." He whispers in my ear.

My mind is slow. When the information finally processes, I lift my head to look at him. "You love me?"

"Yes, Jane. I love you." He kisses me.

I smile at him. I see the love in his eyes. "I love you." I say aloud.

I can feel the shadow that fills my eyes before my brain registers why it is there. He pulls my head back to lay on his chest. *How do you love something you know you cannot keep?*

"Lane."

"Hmm?" He asks.

"I can't stay." I say under my breath.

"I know." He answers. He nearly sounds asleep.

"What do we do?" I ask.

He moves us around on the bed. Covering us with the blankets. Lying on our sides facing each other he says, "I chose to stay with you as long as you are here for me to stay with." He kisses me and pulls me to his chest.

This pain, when it comes, will be the worst pain. This will be the hardest thing to let go of. For me. For him. My mind a tornado of emotions. Different scenarios play in fast forward. All of them end. The pain worse than any broken bones, worse than any loss of life, a pain so deep it could kill us both. I cannot think of this now. Moloch must be sent back. Balance must be returned to this world. Contemplating my own painful misery of life after this will have to wait.

We sleep together.

Twenty Three

The dining room feels different today. The tension, for now, is gone. Everyone seems well rested. Luke and Sara are even in the same room without cross words or side eyes. They also have not spoken to each other, but I will take the win.

Liam nudges Lane. "I'm glad you two finally got some sleep last night. My headphones don't reach a volume loud enough to drown you out." He winks at him.

Lane smacks him away. "Learn to turn it off."

Luke interrupts their banter. "What now?"

"I don't think it's too far out to also consider what will happen after." Lizzie says over her plate. "There are a lot of special people who live in town. They do not know what is coming. Their lives will change abruptly without warning."

"What if we hold a meeting? To warn them." Liam suggests. "We could possibly recruit some help too."

"Beth and I know most of the people in town. Between your connections and our friendly personalities, it could be possible." Lizzie claps in excitement.

A strange bell rings through the house. "What is

that?" I ask.

"The doorbell." Luke says like he cannot believe that I do not know what a doorbell sounds like.

He pushes away from the table and stomps off to answer the door. We all follow behind him. He swings the door open widely. A man dressed in an expensive looking suit stands on the other side. "Vira?"

"Luke." The man opens his arms wide. Luke hugs him back. "Well, are you going to invite me in?"

Luke steps back and announces. "Everyone, our uncle Vira is here."

Liam and Lane meet the man with handshakes and hugs. "Wow! Wearing your marks proudly now, are we? Where are you parents?" He asks taking off his jacket. "And who are these lovely ladies?"

"We are the only ones here right now." Lane says. "This is Sara, Lizzie, Beth, and Jane." He gestures to each of us.

"Nice to meet all of you." He tips his head at us. "Now, I need a drink." He starts walking to the stairs. "When do you expect your parents back?"

Liam rolls his eyes. "Well, we aren't really sure. I will get your scotch. Are you going to the lounge?"

"What? Is that wonderful bartender, what was his name… Steve or something, is he not here?" He continues up the stairs. Luke joins Liam in following behind him.

"I'm sure he is still around. The staff is gone for the day too." Liam explains.

At the top of the stairs Vira stops and looks down on the rest of us. "Why would the staff be gone? A home like this cannot operate without sufficient care." He looks around. "Ah, I see, I have interrupted quite the party." He grins at Liam.

Liam laughs nervously. "No, not anything like that." He clears his throat.

"Don't let me spoil the fun. I could use the entertainment. Come on now, everyone can have a drink." Vira announces and turns off down the hall.

Liam follows close on his heal. Sara is the first of us still standing in the hall to follow them. Lizzie and Beth go behind her. I look at Lane. He shrugs. We go together.

We enter one of the many rooms I have not been in. This room has low, warm, lighting. A few card tables scatter the area. There is an ornate bar tucked in a corner. Fully stocked. A juke box sits on the opposite side of the room from the bar. Most of the seating is club chairs with velvet fabric. All the furniture is a thick, dark wood. With beautifully carved details where it would be most appreciated.

A group of club chairs sits in a circle near the center of the room. A circular rail separates a small circular stage, fully equipped with a pole in the very center.

"Who is getting on the pole?" Vira asks loudly with a cackle. "Calm down. I am just kidding. Clearly none of you fine ladies would know how to work one of these."

I hate him. I can also speak for the other women standing with me. They hate him. Lane looks at me apologetically.

"Vira, we really aren't expecting Kate and Carl home any time soon." Liam says as he stands behind the bar preparing drinks.

"Is there something we can help you with?" Lane asks. Luke flops in one of the chairs in the circle. Sara takes a chair. The rest of us share a look before ultimately sitting around the circle.

"I will wait for my drink to start the hard talk. Tell me, how have things been holding up around here." He looks at Lane.

"You might want to wait on that drink." Lane says.

"That bad huh?" He responds.

"The elders were here." Luke says lamely.

"Did they come to marvel at Lane and all his glory? Look at this man." He shakes Lane's arm as he passes to take the open seat next to him. "I don't think I have ever seen them before. I didn't realize how many you have." He puts a hand beside his mouth in show of telling a secret. "Do they go all the way?" He looks at him pointedly.

Lane clears his throat and shifts in his seat. "Uh, no. No, they didn't come for me."

Liam brings a tray stacked with drinks. "They came for the fallen angel."

He passes drinks around. I start to refuse. He winks at me and a chill-bumps tickle my cheek. He looks pointedly at a particular glass. I take it from the tray and smell it. Club soda. I take a small sip. Just soda. I relax.

Vira grabs the last glass on the tray. He sips it to

taste. "Perfect Liam. Becoming quite the pro at it too." He takes a longer drink. "The fallen angel thing again?"

"Carl has gone off the rails. Edna is dead." Luke spills.

An emotion passes through Vira. The first, other than a boasting confidence since he got here. This one rumbles audibly in my ears. *Rage.*

He controls the emotion well when he talks, "She was quite frail the last time I seen her. Was it at the hand of Carl?" Luke nods. The rage increases. "Anyone else?"

Lane gives Luke a look. Luke ignores it and continues, "Dean, too. Pacha is not dead that we know of, but Edna's death took a toll on her. Supay killed Felicia." I shift in my seat at the mention of her death. Lane takes my hand in his.

"Where are your parents?" Vira asks seriously.

Lane gives Luke another look. "Brock took Carl with him. We left Kate at the tunnel where she tried to have the three of us killed."

"Brock is the one who tried to have you killed. Not Kate." Sara corrects him. Answering some of my own concern on that topic. Brock set up Sara to work out whatever the plan was supposed to be at the tunnels.

Luke jumps up from his seat. I am thankful for the stage blocking him from easily getting to her. "You tried to kill my brothers!" He shouts at her.

"Luke. Sit down." Vira barks.

He ignores him and tries again to explain. "She

took control of my mind…"

"Sit down!" Vira says loudly. He pulls out his phone. Touches the screen a few times then puts it back in his pocket. "Now, it sounds like you all had quite the company. The elite of our people. All here in one place. Without proper protection. Was there a specific reason for this conjuring of power?"

"The fallen angel." Liam repeats.

"We have been looking for this fallen angel, for as long as I can remember. Did we find it?" Vira asks.

"They seem to think so." Lane answers.

"They plan to kill it." Vira remarks.

"There are different opinions on that. Thus, the meeting." Liam answers.

"Thus, the conflict that turned deadly." Luke says over his glass.

"What is the opinion in this lot?" He looks around our group.

"Differences of opinion. We are trying to keep it civil, though. Mostly." Liam answers. He gives Luke a pointed look on the last word.

"There were more of us. They were smart enough to tuck tail and leave." Luke adds.

"They decided that they didn't want to be part of killing someone." Liam defends.

"Seems like they also decided the Fallen's life wasn't worth risking their own to save. Cowards." Vira growls.

"Everyone is free to make their own choices." Lane says.

"Whose choice was it for your marks?" He does not allow Lane time to answer. "When someone is important to you, you make the sacrifices necessary for them." He looks at me. "Yours? Was that your choice? No, it was someone else's. And yet, it hasn't sent you running away from what the consequences are or will be." When no one else says anything he says, "I suggest you all get some rest. I am expecting a guest. I'll take my usual guest bedroom if it is available." Liam stands with him to see him out.

I turn in my seat to Lane. "Was he part of the group of them when they were younger?"

"The group of who?" He asks.

"Felicia told me that many years ago the group of them discovered each other. They once worked together to figure it out, but things started to separate them." I clarify.

"He could have been. I know the elders have known each other for a long time." He tells us.

"How old are you?" I ask him.

"Thirty-one." His lips lift in a smile. "Not too old for you, am I?" He teases.

"No, of course not. Felicia made a strange comment. I guess it wasn't that." I pause. "Can we trust Vira?" I ask.

"He is our uncle." Luke defends him.

"I don't know." Lane answers honestly.

Luke huffs and storms out of the room. The rest of us continue the rest of the day on edge. With someone new in the house the tension returns.

Twenty Four

The doorbell wakes us the next morning. Everyone ends up in the hall again, waiting to see who is on the other side. Vira made it to the door first. He does not swing the door wide. We all crane our necks to try to get a peek. He turns to look at each of us.

"To the dining room with you all. I will bring our guest for introductions momentarily." We all follow his order.

The atmosphere is tense as we all sit at the table waiting for the door to open. We left the head of the table and the seat to its right empty for Vira and the mystery guest. We take all the first seats to the left side of the head seat. Liam, Luke, Lane, Me, Lizzie, Beth, and Sara. In that order.

Vira comes through the door first, then his guest. Instantly I recognize him. I look to the others to see if they do too. Vira sits at the head. His guest takes the third seat on the right side. Putting himself directly across from Lane. A primal anger rises inside me. The primal feeling from before. Before I thought it was sexual tension, but now I know it is about territory. He is a threat. His green eyes shine in my direction. His face, the same one I look at every day, only it is not covered in the beautiful tattoos.

He is Lane's father.

He is, "Moloch." I say his name aloud before Vira can introduce him. The room tenses. Moloch smiles.

Vira starts to protest. Moloch holds a single finger at him. "You cannot charm this one." He says with a grin on his face. The sound of his voice sends chills down my neck. The heat of my anger quickly washing the sensation away. "Seems I have finally gotten what I wanted, Chaska." He watches me for a moment. "It took coming to this world to gain my victory and a very long way about things, but here it is now." He looks up and down the table. "You all seem very confused." He looks at Vira. "Let's get some food in here. I have quite the story to tell."

"We don't need to hear anything you have to say." I spit the words at him through my teeth.

"Chaska, darling. The rumors are true then. Your memories are damaged. Possibly even gone." He leans back in his chair. "Of course, they are true. I am hurt that you treat me this way now."

"It is not easy to sit here." I hiss.

"None of that matters now. I have succeeded. My blood line is finally meshed with yours. Our descendants will be the most powerful things in all the worlds." He smiles. Proud of himself.

Vira pushes back in with a large tray. He sets it in the center of the table. Moloch is the only one who starts piling his plate with food. He talks as he takes a bite. "You see it took some very smart humans to help me with my dilemma. It took many attempts. There were about seventy-five. I only needed one. One and the right balance of chemicals to hold you in place until he was fully matured. These humans dream of things I am able to accomplish. They dream of growing children where their own bodies and circumstances have failed. They dream of youth everlasting. They dream of knowledge. I have it all. They will bow at my feet to have a taste."

"I will stop you." I growl.

"Look at him." He looks at Lane. "We created him. We were able to make him without worry of the host's genetics interfering with his design. You see, that was the trouble in the beginning. We had so many halflings that had to be disposed of. A couple, I did grow fond of, I almost kept but they were disposed of when I was sure we had a successful specimen." He admires Lane like a piece of art. Lane's body seems about to explode as Moloch continues talking. "Vira suggested having him raised by humans. He would be more likely to find you, the less I was involved. It worked perfectly. These markings of art were not in my plans, but they do not affect the ability to send me through the generations, so mute it be. So, I sat back, let lose the spirits and gave passage for some of ours. The rest found its way." He leans forward and toward me leaning his arms on the table. "Chaska, you can't stop me here. Besides, you are family now, you have a home here with your family. I do hope for a grandson."

I stand up too fast for the chair. It crashes to the floor behind me. "My name is not Chaska." I storm out. I can feel Lane close on my heels. I slam the back door open and stomp across the grounds to the willow tree.

Twenty Five

At the tree, I break down. I crumple to my knees with sobs rocking my body. Lane wraps me in his arms. "I couldn't sit in there a second longer." I mumble through sobs.

"I think we are all thankful for the excuse to get out of there." He says to me. Around him, the rest of our little group hovers.

The sobs pass and I wipe my face on my sleeve. Sara asks, "Do we believe what he was saying?"

"Either way, I bet he knows what you can do, how do we stop him?" Liam asks.

"Brute force isn't going to work on him. If he were worried about that, he wouldn't have shown up." Luke adds.

"Vira had to have let him know that it was just us. Maybe that is why he came first. To judge his opposition." Lizzie says.

"Do you remember anything about him from before?" Lane asks.

"No. Not before the night at the club. But I know what he is saying is mostly true. I cannot put together anything solid. I just know." I pause and look at the trunk of the willow. "We have to be smart about our next series of actions. I think I need a while alone. To think." I do not meet any of their eyes. They all leave from the cover of the branches. Lane hugs me into him before following the others.

I face the tree, my legs folded under me. If I am going to send him back, I need to find out where that is. I drop my head and place both hands against the trunk. Willing it to lead me home. Nothing seems to change until I hear a soft voice.

"Chaska? Chaska!" The sound gets louder, and I hear footsteps hitting the ground fast. I turn to see a beautiful woman approaching me. She is dressed in a long gown that is a pale yellow. Her feet are bare. Her hair hangs in long, golden, waves held back from her face with a thin swirl of a silver metal. "Chaska, where have you been?"

I look around myself. I am in a garden. One hand still placed on the trunk of a tree. The trunk matches the twisted look of the willow but the branches on this tree reach out towards the sky. "Where am I?" I ask.

"Aymara. Do you not recognize your own home?" The woman asks. Another woman materializes beside me. She came from inside me. Sara's power. The woman looks at me strangely. Her features change and she runs away from me. "Has something happened?" The first woman asks, watching the other run off in the distance.

"How do I bring Moloch back here?" Keep focused on the mission. I tell myself. I do not have time to explain things to this person. I do not have time to linger here and savor in its beauty. I do not know how long being here will take me from being with Lane.

"Moloch is with you?" She nearly yells. "Pachacutec will not be pleased. Catch him and transport him here. Now!" She demands.

"How do I do that?" I beg.

"You have been crossing realms too long. Get him to this gateway. You know the fate that waits for you." A tear falls down her cheek. "He will not show mercy. We all know the price for such defiance." She scolds me.

"How long have I been gone?" I ask.

"Go! Before he sees you." She shoves me back to the tree. I barely touch it and I am back under my willow.

I rush from under her branches to find the others. They are there walking toward the manor. Liam turns around first. "Well, that was fast."

"I didn't learn much, but I know what I have to do. Your long game plan needs to be put in motion." I explain.

"We didn't really discuss that." Sara says.

"We should now." I say to her. I lead on to the manor. Vira is lingering in the hall when we walk in. As if he has been watching us through the windows to the backyard. "Where is Moloch?" I ask him.

"He has been waiting on you in the convention hall." He gestures widely with his arms to go ahead.

Inside, Moloch is lounging in one of the thrones. Tina and Tracy flank him. They are gagged and bound standing upright. "You ran out so quickly I didn't have a chance to tell you, your friends are here."

Someone enters from behind the stage area. Pacha and Supay take seats in the thrones. I decide that now is a good a time as any to start this long game. "You seem to know more about me than I know of myself. I have no memories of how I got here or where I came from. I am sorry I reacted so strongly. This has all been very frustrating."

Moloch shifts in his chair. "What are you saying?"

I think about protecting my friends. Shielding their minds from him. I feel the ripple in the air pass by either side of me. "I really can't be sure." I say honestly. "I don't want to see anyone else get hurt. These two," I gesture at Tina and Tracy, "have betrayed me many times recently. If you think torturing them will in turn torture me, you are wrong. Supay killed the only person I was truly close to before I found this group. I am finding it difficult not to attack him here and now. But this is not what I want. I do not want to fight for things I do not understand. I don't want people to suffer due to my ignorance." I pause for a long moment. I feel my friend's emotions ripple around me. "Teach me." I finally say.

"I have to say, this is not what I expected." He stands. He rubs his hands together. Turns on his heel forcefully. Facing the others. "See, where we come from traitors are handled quickly and swiftly."

"Here doesn't have to be that way." I say to his back. Desperate to stop what he is about to do.

"I understand that your human form does not understand this part. Though I can feel how much you love my son and that the love I crave from you still evades me, I understand that I will never be formerly at your side." He pauses, his back still to us. He holds back something else he wants to say. His shoulders broaden with a deep breath. "It is still my duty to serve and protect my queen." His hands reach out toward Tina and Tracy. Each one hovers inches away from their throats. Supay stands. "Sit, this is my honor." He barks at him. Tina and Tracy begin gasping for air behind their gags. I am frozen. Unable to move. Their struggles slow. Their faces stark white. Then stillness.

    Moloch turns back toward me. A wild look in his eyes. He closes the short distance between us, stopping just inches away. "No one will betray you again, my love." My skin crawls. "No one leaves the property. I will take a leave now. Clean this up." He says to all of us. He leaves in a streak of speed.

    Supay carries the bodies of Tina and Tracy. One under each arm. I am surprised by his strength. Pacha follows him out. My friends look to me for answers. Confusion and fear ripples all around us.

    I do not have any answers for them. This all happened so fast. I cannot even process my own feelings about my former best friends being murdered in front of me. Their bodies taken away. I am frozen in shock and fear. Other pieces of information start to fall into place in my mind. If Supay and Pacha are here and they somehow had Tina and Tracy, Brock must be here too. Kyle. Do we even know how many other people are in Brock's clan?

    I take a deep breath. I pull my eyes away from the empty stage area in front of me. The group around me waiting for me to say something. Anything.

Twenty Six

"We can't stay here." Lane barks. He is pacing the long length of the dining room table. "Not if they are here. We should leave now."

"Please tell me this is part of your long game plan." Sara pleads.

In a low voice I begin explaining. "If we meet him with force, he will kill every one of you. He will not kill me, but that is the problem. My main goal must be to take him back. With as few casualties as possible."

"Did you find out how to do that?" Lizzie asks hopefully.

"I am from Aymara. I have a father there and I think a sister. The willow connects our worlds. Time is different there. They have not begun searching for me. They did not know Moloch was here too. It seems urgent to them that Moloch be returned." I tell them. "Getting him to the other side will be the easy part. Getting him to the willow will be the hard part. More so if he knows what the willow is. I have to find a way for him to trust me. Just long enough to get the job done."

"He will fight us if he finds out that plan." Lizzie

says.

"Is it safe for us to be talking about this here?" Beth whispers.

"Probably not. This should be the last time we discuss the plan in any amount of detail. He is able to sense when we are using our powers." I look at Liam. "I am going to trust in all of you to do what you think is best. Try not to resist him but also don't make it obvious."

"How long do you think this will take?" Luke asks.

"Days, weeks, possibly even months. I don't imagine he trusts easily." I answer.

"Everyone is ok with this? Just walk around and make friends with the enemy. And trust each other that we have not switched sides. I don't know if I can do this." Liam says.

"For now, this is the plan." Lane answers. "Now if you don't mind, I want to go rest." He stands. He does not talk to me. I follow him out.

∞∞∞

In his room he sits on the sofa in the changing area. His fingers folded in front of him. His elbows resting on his knees. I let him sit in silence.

"Are you pregnant?" He asks. Breaking the silence.

"I don't know." I answer.

"He talks like you are." He retorts.

"Yes. Dean mentioned it too." I respond. I take a deep breath. "Whether it is true or not, is not important. We have to follow the plan."

"The plan is barely a thing. If you are, then you shouldn't be putting yourself in danger." He has not looked at me.

"One life is not more important than the many. I am the only one who can take him back. I cannot let selfish excuses distract me from that." I say to him.

"This is not a selfish excuse. This affects more than just you." He snaps at me.

"I get it, the promise of life, a future, a family is appealing. Bringing a child in to a world with enemies and misbalanced powers is not fair to that child. A life of fear and constant battle is not a life I will pass on to any generation. This has to stop here, Lane." I try to reason with him. "Besides, at max it would be only a week or two in motion. How would anyone even know yet?"

"Are you considering abortion then?" He spits at me.

"No. That is not it at all." I think about my words. "I will not allow myself to grow attached to something that may not be true or be possible for me. I think you should also be ready for that. We do not understand enough of what is to come. What if I die? What if I must stay on the other side when I take Moloch? What if the things I have to do become too much for a growing life?"

"It is called hope. I don't see anything wrong with having hope." He is calmer now.

"What if it isn't human? There could be enough of me and whatever Moloch has done that it also can't stay here." I try to reason with him. "It could have enough of you that it can't survive where I am from."

"We don't know if any of that is true." He argues.

"Lane, I will do what is necessary to stop Moloch." I feel myself giving into him. "I will do it mindfully though. I will try my best to let it grow, if it is even there, I will not put myself in a position of danger if I can help it at all."

"What would he do with it, if it's real?" He asks.

"Whatever the outcome of this, he will not do anything with it." I respond strongly. If a baby comes from this, it will not know anything about Moloch. Not his name nor what he looks like.

"Am I even supposed to be alive?" He nearly whispers.

I drop to floor in front of him. Sitting on my knees. I take both of his hands. "I can't even start to understand all of the things he told us. This world has a way of making things right. I do know that I love you. And that is real. And right."

"How much of that is by our choice? Is it the part of me that he created?" He looks like he is going to keep asking questions.

"I love you." I pull his face to look at me.

"I've been having nightmares." He admits. "In them, I join him. Some part inside of me thinks I belong at his side. In the beginning I am always fighting him off. By the end, he has won."

"You won't. I won't let you." I say to him. "They are probably caused by the confusing information. Your brain is trying to rationalize everything that contradicts what we thought we knew."

He shakes his head and looks away from me. "I don't think that is it." He pauses. "What if I am not supposed to be here either? I don't belong in Aymara either."

"I don't remember enough about Aymara to know if that is a possibility. I am sorry I do not have the answers. This thing we are doing now, it is the right thing, I know that for sure. I can only work with that right now. Get Moloch back to Aymara. Return balance to the spiritual realm." I tell him the short, but concrete, version of the plan that only half exists.

Twenty Seven

I was hesitant to leave, but Lane insisted that he just needed a little space. A shower and some real rest would help his mood, he told me. I stand in the hall outside his bedroom door. I want to slam it back open and demand that I stay with him. Tell him that I will help him through these emotions he is feeling. But then, I remember that when I needed a moment to myself, he went without arguing. He let me have that space. When I was done, he was there when I was ready. I clinch my fists and will myself to give him this time.

"Psst." Liam is at the other end of the hall. He waves me to join him. "He is just being stubborn. He could be right; a little rest will help ease his mind. He is being an asshole in his head too. If you need reassurance that it isn't just toward you." He puts and arm over my shoulder as he guides me to the entertainment room.

"Is everyone else in there?" I ask before he opens the door.

"Nah, I thought you could use a little space from everything too." He says with a grin. Then taps on his temple.

Inside I grab a glass of soda and find a seat near a corner of the room. "Do you have any questions about what is happening?" I ask him. I cannot fool myself; I do not want to be alone right now.

"Probably a million or so. Only one question matters though." He reaches in his back pocket. He holds out a small rectangular box. "Maybe 'matters' is the wrong word, but this is an 'easy to answer' question. That may even help."

I take the slightly crushed box. It is mostly pink with large print scattered all over the front of it. 'Early response' and 'six days sooner' printed in bold writing. "What if it makes everything much worse?" I can hear the desperation in my voice.

"There is a small bathroom right over there. I will be here when you finish." He promises.

I should be mad at him for assuming this is what we should be concerned about right now. Pushing me to take one of these things when we have a battle headed our way. I cannot be mad though. He knows what is in my head. He probably has the right idea. This one thing has a straightforward way to get a definite answer. I worry though, even with the claims of early response and six days sooner, is it too soon for this thing to even give a correct answer?

I open the box as I make my way to the door Liam gestured towards. I pull out the folded paper of directions. I scan through it quickly. 'Pee on it. Wait three minutes. Results.' Seems simple enough. Too simple for an answer that could rock the very earth I stand on. I do as the directions tell. Place the cap on the end that is grossly covered in my urine. Place it on the counter of the small sink. And wait.

Three minutes pass over an eternity. I wait one more just to be safe. My knees go stiff from standing still for too long. I start to peddle them out. In the small space I nearly knock the test off the counter. I look at it accidentally. Two lines. *Two lines?* I do not remember if I read in the directions about what the lines meant. I kick myself for not paying attention on the pages that described this part. I dig through the small bin of trash for the crumpled paper. I scan through looking for the words 'two lines,' it takes two flips of the paper for my brain to finally register any words on the page. Finally, 'two lines is a positive pregnancy test.' My stiff knees go weak, and I am sitting in the floor of the small bathroom reading the words over and over again.

I flinch at the knock on the door even though it is a quiet tap, tap. "You should come out here and sit with me." Liam's voice comes muted through the wooden door.

I know he already knows. I know that is all my mind can think about right now. Even if he were not looking for it, he would probably still hear it. Slowly I gather myself. I shove the used test in my pocket. I am caught off guard when I open the door and suddenly there are large arms wrapped around me. Holding my head to his chest. Then it happens, my body shivers once, my tears stain his shirt, and then my chest rocks with sobs. I sink into his chest. He pets my head. He holds me like this for a long time. Not saying anything, not moving, until the rocking in my chest settles and the sobs grow quiet.

"How the hell could I have been so careless? I don't remember my past, but I have definitely been around long enough to know better than this."

"Now, now, don't be so hard on yourself." He guides me back to the chair I originally sat in. He tops off my drink then takes the chair opposite me. "Lane wants this. He is struggling with himself over it. He knows he shouldn't." He pauses. "It doesn't have to be such a terrible thing." Liam says.

"I just found out that I can't stay here. What kind of coparenting is that going to look like? Time to go to Earth to see your dad for Christmas or, time to go to your mom's world for summer." The sarcasm is thick in my tone.

"We don't know that that isn't possible. We also don't know that you have to leave." He tries to reason with me. Without me having to word it aloud he says, "Maybe you do have to go." He puts his hands up in surrender.

"Before that is all even close to being discussed though, I have to put every spirit back in its place. I must take back all the spirits from my world. Those are the ones I must physically carry within me. Can she live through that? Will my body be able to carry both?" I kick myself for calling it a 'she.'

Liam notices and grins. "You know more about her than you are letting yourself see." He leans forward in his chair. "You can sense her like He can."

"Knowing it doesn't make anything easier." I glare.

"Take a deep breath and just think about her for a moment." Liam says softly.

I stand from my chair. "Liam, I cannot do that. There is a chance that sh… it will not survive. I don't need the distraction or the disappointment." I stomp out of the room.

Before the door slams, he shouts, "I won't tell him, but you should."

Twenty Eight

Needing space of my own. I left Liam in the game room. I have been wandering since then. I strolled the quiet halls. Found my way outside where the blackened mark still scars the ground. It is amazing how quickly new life has started to repair the damage. Small, green buds scatter the surface of the destruction left by me. This world heals itself. I am comforted at the thought. No matter what damage I have caused, it will recover from this. Why I came here in the first place, I still do not know.

I have continued wandering until now. I stand just outside the branches of the willow. I cannot convince myself to go under her cover. I cannot seem to make myself go back inside with the others. So, I stand. Not inside. Not outside. In the middle. Where I wish I could just stay. The middle would be a happy place. My being here on this earth has caused pain. My leaving this earth will cause pain. Either way I lose, but Lane loses the most. I hope that a healing process starts just as fast for him as it has for the earth.

My cheek freezes pulling me away from my pity party for one. I dash back to the manor. When I make it to the back door of the main hall Liam crashes down the stairs toward the front side of the long hall.

"The convention hall!" He shouts as he darts across the hall.

It takes me much longer to cover the distance of the long hall. I nearly skid past the door to go in. I hear a loud crash from inside. I throw the door open. Liam is in a heap to my left.

At the front Moloch stands over a crumpled body. *Lane.* My heat explodes through me. "Calm down, Chaska. I wouldn't kill my favorite son."

"Get away from him." I growl.

"I know he is very confused. I will forgive him for this. This time." He pauses. He turns his attention to Liam. Still in a heap on the floor. "The others though are disposable to me. You should advise them not to attack me if you don't want them dead." When I do not move, he barks, "Call your friends, I have made a decision about how our futures will look."

I take two steps toward Lane and him. "You can help your other friend. My son stays with me."

It takes a few attempts to get Liam to open his eyes. He starts to panic, ready to fight again. "Let's get everyone else first." I whisper to him.

We quickly find everyone else. "He has Lane. I don't know what happened." I explain in a rush.

"Lane tried to confront him. He was hiding his mind from me. I didn't see in time to stop him." Liam explains over Lizzie who is at his side, healing him.

She stands and brushes her hands off. "A mild concussion. Easy fix. You are good to go."

"Are we scrapping the plan yet?" Luke growls.

"No. He won't kill Lane, but he will kill all of you. We still need to be smart about our moves. He wants us back in the convention hall. Keep your tempers and reactions in check." I explain to them.

"He may not kill Lane, but he has no problem hurting him." Liam says between his teeth. I worry for Lane. If Liam is this mad, Lane could really be hurt.

"I don't know if I can control my anger." Luke says under his breath. I know what he says is true.

"I called Dave and Miley." Sara blurts. We all look at her. "They didn't say for sure that they would come back, but they didn't say no either. I knew they would want to know that He is here."

"One thing at a time." I say before turning to lead everyone into the convention room. *I hate this room.*

∞∞∞

Lane is seated in one of the throne-like chairs next to Moloch. Relief washes over me that he is no longer in a heap on the floor. Vira, Supay, and Pacha fill the other chairs. One chair next to Lane sits empty.

"Please, everyone, take a seat." Moloch says. None of us move. "Sit." He barks.

Liam nudges my arm. I sit first, the rest of them file down the row of chairs placed in front of Moloch. "What a crowd?" He grins.

I look at each of the elders facing us. The air ripples around Vira. It does not come close enough for me to tell what he is using his power on. Or even what power he has. Pacha glares at us. Supay looks bored. Lane is sitting stark still. His gaze fixed on a single point somewhere behind us.

"I found these two approaching the property." He gestures toward the left side.

Brock leads Dave and Miley to stand in the open space between our two facing rows. *I did not know Brock was back.* Does he have people watching the property? Dave and Miley look ashamed.

"I invited these two." He gestures to the right side of the room.

Kyle leads Carl and Kate to stand beside the others. Carl stands, too proud. Kate has a stone expression glued in place on her face. Brock stays near Dave and Miley. Kyle moves to one of the empty thrones in line.

"These two," he looks to Dave and Miley, "are they friends of yours?"

"Yes." I answer.

"Did you call them to spy on me?" He asks. His voice pitching on the end, pointedly.

I do not know the right answer here. "No. I called for backup." The closest thing to the truth that I could get without sending my friends under the bus.

"Hmph. Well, you can have them. Your numbers mean nothing next to my power. So, if this is what makes you happy." Brock shoves the two of them near chairs in our line. They sit looking relieved. Brock takes a throne in the other line. The throne next to Lane is still empty.

Moloch stands and walks a slow circle around Carl and Kate. "The two of you were chosen to raise my son." Carl smiles proudly. Kate's face does not change. "Then you tried to kill my son," he stops in front of Carl, "and then my queen." He continues his walk around until he arrives back in front of Kate. She barely flinches, if I were not staring, I would have missed it. "You allowed all this and the mutilation of my son's skin." He continues walking again. He ends his circling and sits back in his throne. "Supay."

Supay's face wrinkles in a sickening smile. Carl's smile fades from his face. A tear escapes Kate's eye. Supay slowly makes his way to them.

"Don't do this." I bark, jumping up from my seat.

Moloch gives me a sideways look. "You protect this man after he made attempts to kill you?"

"He is the father of my friends. Imprisonment or banishment would be more suiting for his crimes." My voice sounds strange in my ears. A memory swirls in my brain. I push it aside for now. "No more death." I finish.

"And, what say you about her." He points at Kate.

"She has been heavily influenced by the people around her and we think she may have even been under mind control during some of that." I tell him.

"Ah ha." He exclaims, "You have a… what do you call it?" He looks at Vira.

"Mind walker." Vira's answer is short. He is focusing awfully hard on something. I can still see the air rippling around him.

"Yes, mind walker. You have one amongst you?" Moloch asks.

"Not any longer." I answer.

"So, you have taken life." He says with a grin.

"No, I have not." I snap back at him.

He looks at me for a long while. He reads my face. I quickly think of protecting my friends. I kick myself for not already doing it.

"You took it." He says under his breath. He facial expression changes around the very edges of his eyes.

This is not good. I did not realize he did not know. I push to protect my friends from him. I even include Carl and Kate. Something is blocking me from Lane. I have suspicions that may be Vira's doings. He may be their mind walker.

"What would you have me do with them?" He changes the topic. His expression returns to his normal look of confidence.

"Imprisonment. Here with us. Limited to the grounds." I answer faster than anyone expected. "Much like my own imprisonment." I finish with a hiss.

"This is all for your protection from others like them." He growls as he jams a finger toward Carl and Kate.

"Then I welcome them under my same protection." I counter. I know they are one of my enemies. I also made a promise of no more death.

"I will make you a deal." He says after a moment of thought. "My son seems to believe that you don't want to keep the child. I offer you a trade of life for lives. You keep the child, and I will kill no one else."

He waits for my response. "What is the catch?" I ask suspiciously.

"All that I would like in return is some bonding time with my son. He will need to learn all about us before he can raise my grandchild." He explains.

My face tingles along my tattoo. Liam seems to believe this is a promising idea. Lane has not reacted to anything happening around him. The ripple of air still surrounds Vira. If I agree to this, Lane gets the child he wants, all the killing stops, and Moloch gets to spread his radical ideologies. *Will I be able to keep Lane from turning into another Moloch?* My cheek tingles again. I cast Liam a sharp look.

"You are also welcome to join us." He gestures to the empty seat. "Help us to lead the future of our kind." Carl had said something similar to this before.

My tattoo tingles. "Fine. I will not join you. I agree to trade a life for lives." I answer Moloch.

He looks pleased with this response.

Twenty Nine

"We will be on our way then." Moloch announces. Supay, Pacha, Brock and Kyle all leave through the back exit. Vira guides Lane to follow the first three. Moloch nods to us. "We will be back when the baby has arrived."

"What?" I yell. The real catch. He intends for us to stay put while he takes Lane away.

"I cannot bond with my son with so much distraction. Between his brothers, and that child he would never learn to trust me. Of course, we will take our leave and return when our presence is once again required." He follows the others through the rear exit without any more explanation.

I jump to my feet. One big arm comes around my middle, stopping me from pursuing them. Liam spins me to face him.

"We have to trust that Lane will be able to handle this." He hears the question in my head before I can voice it. "No, I can't hear him. I haven't been able to since he came in here originally."

"Then what makes you think he will be able to handle this?" I challenge. "He is not in control. Do you know what Vira can do?" I demand.

"No." Liam says dropping his head.

Lizzie walks up to us and puts a hand on my arm. "This has a silver lining. We can train freely. We will have about eight months or more to live without threat. This may give us an opening to take Moloch out. He sounds like he is excited for this child. This could be his weakness. Our opportunity." She looks at me expectantly.

She is right about that. Carl interrupts my thoughts, "I could eat."

Liam's arm drops away from me. No longer worried that I will run. I look toward the exit where Lane went, seemingly willing, with Moloch.

I gather myself before turning to Carl. Luke and Liam are angry at him. Sara has tucked herself as far in her seat as she can get. "Your imprisonment will be strictly enforced. This is your second chance. Any more behaviors like before and you will be met with a fast verdict and your next sentence will be death." He nods. I gesture for him to leave. I hope he does not call my bluff. I would not be able to sentence someone to death.

Kate looks down at her hands. "I don't know exactly what part you played in all of this. This is also your second chance with the same consequences as his." I say to her. She nods. "You will have a job though. We need someone who understands how to run this manor. I know nothing of what it takes to pay and hire staff or to make sure the house is sufficiently supplied. This will be your duty to save any of us from having to learn how and then do it. We will need to be focused on other important tasks. Is this something you are already familiar with?" I ask her.

"Yes. It was my main job before." She answers quietly. The confidence that she once had seems to be gone now. I am sad for her.

"That's great. If you will make the necessary arrangements to hire back the staff, that would be greatly appreciated." I gesture for her to go on.

"Way to take lead, boss." I hear the snark in Miley's tone.

"Honestly, I am just trying not to fall apart right now." I respond to her.

I am wound tight. I want to run after Lane. Bring him back. Fix whatever Moloch has done to him. They are all right. I need to trust that Lane will be able to handle Moloch. We need to be ready for when they come back. Training should be top priority.

Sara walks over to Miley and Dave. "I will get them caught up. Maybe you should get some rest." She says to me in an easy voice.

"I think that is a great idea." Lizzie chimes in. She glances up at Liam and smiles. She places a gentle hand on his forearm.

She loops her arm through mine and guides me out of this wretched room. We walk in silence to Lane's room. Liam and she shared a moment back there. I am sure of it. I have been so caught up in my own problems that I have not noticed a romance brewing between them.

They all have, for the most part, stood by my every

decision. Without question. I have been selfish. Taking every crisis as a personal attack that I have not considered their lives. The impact this must be taking on them. We have not slowed down to mourn the loss of the people around us. No pause to rest before something else happens. A new threat. A spin of events marking nearly every day.

Liam and Luke were both against me in the beginning. At some point they both switched, even if Luke can sometimes be difficult. Sara did horrible, unforgivable things to them both, yet she walks among us because I forgave her for them. Lizzie has taken my side at every turn. No hesitation. Beth, well, I do not know that I have ever had a conversation more than a couple sentences long with her. She is more loyal to Lizzie than me, but that does not make less of her presence. Miley and Dave agreed not to fight against me. They may have left but this fight has brought them back. Against their will.

They are not here for me. I am not the tie that is holding us together. It is all of us. Liam's tie to me, belief in me, is unavoidable with the link of the tattoo. Luke is here for Liam. A brotherly bond, unbreakable. Lizzie could be here for Liam as well, though I am not sure if that is what originally kept her or if that grew because she stayed. Beth to Lizzie. Sara stays for fear of what her life before would do to her now. Dave and Miley came back because of her call. I am only a commonality between them.

I cannot pinpoint when this all came to be. I do not even think I could figure it out going back through chronological order. I cannot leave it like this. Lane started the *'everyone deserves to have a choice in their fate'* thing. I have even preached it since then. But that is not what has happened in practice. I owe it to them to change that.

Even the elders made me feel like I was the center of attention. That also has not always been true. They were once a group of people with similar interests that at some point split them apart. This is where Moloch has gained a power hold on all of us. By setting us against each other. I doubt he wants to bond with Lane. Lane barely seemed conscious to the things happening around him. No, Moloch knows that taking Lane away from not only me, but also his brothers and his friends, he gains the upper hand of having something we all care for. Something we will most likely have opposing opinions on how to correct. He has the knife that could slice us all apart without him lifting a finger.

Moloch is a manipulator. Everything that has led us to this point, I think he has carefully crafted to work out this way. He is smart or at least has surrounded himself with smart people. I may not remember where we come from or how we got here, but I think I have put together what happened.

He was the one who created the pills that I was taking. Directly or indirectly, he made sure Tracy befriended me and supported my addiction. Before that, he claims that he created Lane. Even farther back then that he befriended Dean.

Dean was full of information that we missed the opportunity to take advantage of. Moloch said he released the spirits, maybe the group of elders were some of the first to obtain these powers. He could have used Dean the way he is clearly using Vira.

Vira is a mind walker. Dean seemed to read my mind when I was communicating with Liam. Mind walkers are our biggest threat. Moloch talked about giving people youth and Felicia had mentioned Supay being over two-hundred years old. Could any of that be possible?

I force myself to get into Lane's bed. I could theorize all night and never come to any solutions. A cool breeze brushes across my face. My imagination. The shadow of Lane's existence here, haunting me. Sleep does not come easily.

Thirty

I wake up early to beat everyone else to the dining room. A few staff members have already shown up today. I am surprised at how quickly Kate was able to get them to return. Each one that I pass, smiles broadly. Some even hum 'good morning.' Their eagerness to return to work beams from every inch of them. Another type of misfortune caused by me. Whoever made the decision to send them away, rocked their very beings. Their lively hoods pulled from under them without warning. I return each of their smiles and thank each one of them for returning so promptly.

In the kitchen I find two more staff members preparing breakfast. I help them for a while. I send one of the others to let everyone know what time the food will be served. I set the table myself. The way I had watched Kate before. Crossing the hall between the dining room and kitchen, I think I see the shadow of someone.

I call out, "Who is there?". No one answers. I move down the hall to check hidden corners. No one is there.

It is just my eyes playing tricks on me with the rising sun through the windows. A lingering paranoia that I cannot seem to shake settles. I try to assure myself that we are safe. I miss Lane deeply enough that I could be fooling myself. Expecting him to suddenly return.

I take the head of the table and wait as the others trickle in. They look at me expectantly. "You seem to have been busy already this morning." Liam teases.

"Let's eat." I announce when Luke, the last one to join us, sits.

The motions are slow and calculated at first. After a few bites, the mood at the table lightens. Small talk passes across and up and down the table. As eating slows, I get down to the significant business of calling them all here.

"Thank you so much for being here. I have not been fair to all of you recently. I have accepted your help. Expected it really." I admit. "I have not purposely taken control of the rhetoric. Yet, that is exactly what has happened. Today, that all changes. A decision will not be made without careful consideration from all of you." I say with resolve.

Kate kindly interrupts, "Should Carl and I be here for this?" She starts to push away from the table.

"You both should stay. This will most definitely have an impact on your futures. You deserve, at the very least, to know what is coming. With time maybe even a say." I look around the table. Each face is lost in thought. "It was not fair of me to speak on your behalf's. It was not fair of me to have you all trapped in here with me. Giving up whatever lives you may have had. Being stuck here does not mean you are expected to train or fight. If you choose not to, I will not ask it of you again. Two things I would like to bring to the table first and foremost." I take a deep breath. "I made a decision yesterday to allow Carl to walk freely amongst us. Do any of you at all have any challenges for that?" I ask them collectively.

Liam, understanding my approach, speaks first. "I think this arrangement works. As long as the understanding of harsher punishment for future offenses is taken seriously." Everyone else nods at this in agreement.

I accept that as answer enough and move to my next question. "Next, I appointed Kate to taking care of the house. Any challenges for that?"

Luke and Liam both say no right away. Clearly, they do not want to do her job. "If I could, I'd like to shadow her some. Maybe check over her as well. I would like to learn what it takes to make a home of this size operate." Beth says. Her voice the loudest I have ever heard it reach.

"I think that would be a great idea. Anyone disagree?" I ask the table. Lizzie smiles at Beth. Pride beaming from her.

"I must warn you it is a lot more work than you might think." Kate says with a grin. She seems to look forward to having someone to mentor.

"Does anyone else have any immediate topics to bring up?" Everyone sits silent, considering.

"It is important to find out, now, who is willing to train. Of course, with the choice to join in later, or even drop out, always being available." Lizzie says to the group. A lot of nods in agreement around the table. "It will also help to have scheduled training times. Once we know who is interested."

"Hold that thought. I want to grab one of my ledgers from the office. We should be organized." Kate pushes away from the table. She waits for a nod from me before continuing out.

"We can't leave." Miley states.

"I know." I respond.

Before I can say anything else, she looks at me seriously. "We physically cannot leave the property. I went on my morning…" she clears her throat, "jog. There is a barrier trapping us in. The hired help seems to be able to cross it. I cannot and Dave cannot. I am sure the rest of us can't either." She finishes.

Kate pushes back through the door. A large black book tucked under her arm, a laptop, and a handful of pens. She breaks the silence that has settled around Miley's discovery. "What do we plan first?"

We start with deciding who is going to train for battle. Beth moves to a seat next to Kate, together they start jotting down notes. The two of them are the only ones who decide not to train. It is voted on that Carl be allowed to observe. Until he can earn back some of our trust. A training schedule is decided on. One that will not overwork any one person and give us the opportunity to match with opposing and similar powers. Against each other and working together. No more than five days a week and no more than two training session per person per day. A larger, general exercise, session will be held on weekdays. Weekends will be a time for rest. Our agreed upon focus is stamina. If we can last longer than them, we have a better chance of tiring them out.

We set up an emergency plan for staff members. Beth gets them filled in on all the details. We want them to know what could be coming. No more surprises. They are each given the chance to decide for themselves. So far, all of them have made the decision to stay. Their loyalty is greatly appreciated, but I know it is not to any of us at this table. Their loyalties are to their families and continuing a career they have come accustom to.

In attempt to show allegiance, Carl gives us information. The elders were once just like us. Only, in their day, they believed they were the only ones who had any powers. They set up things just like we are now. Planning and training. The original group consisted of Vira, Dean, Brock, and Carl. Felicia came to them early on. Searched them out. "Her crazy ass came all the way here to battle us. Alone." He laughs when he remembers that.

They were not interested in fighting anyone at the time. They were young boys who could do amazing things. They wanted to *'pick up chicks'*, is how he explains it. Showing off was apparently how he won Kate's heart. Dean met Edna, who was a beautiful warrior even if she was much older than any of them. She then led them to Supay and Pacha. Where things changed.

Their group started to tear at the seams. Egos and opinions. They went their separate ways. Later coming to agreements to hold meetings. More people started getting powers. The gifts were being passed through genetics to children. They could work together as separate clans. Support their kind and have different opinions. That is the way life works in this world already.

"Jealousy changed me." He admits. "The one thing

we all agreed on was that Moloch was the first of our kind. Dean worked right next to him. His right-hand-man. I wanted that position. More than anything else in the world." Sadness fills his eyes. He looks at Kate. She takes his hand in hers.

I believe him. I still do not trust him, and there is much that has been left out of this story. I cannot help my suspicion. Before we close the meeting, I add, "Moloch has to be returned to Aymara. From what I understand, I am the only one who can take him back." I take a deep breath. "All of the powers that are here on earth, I have to take those away too." I pause. "I won't do that until I am sure Moloch is securely on the other side."

Liam stands. "If a person uses their powers against you or any of us, I vote you take their power without delay. No second chances, no trial. You take it." His voice is strong and demanding. We all feel it rumble through the air. Everyone agrees.

The meeting ends.

Thirty One

Five thousand one hundred hours and twenty-eight minutes. The time that has passed since Lane was taken away. Life here has fallen into routine. Morning breakfast, everyone is there. A time to bring latest information or new topics to vote on. Mostly we socialize all together. The last major thing we voted on was new curtains in the sunroom. We train according to our schedules. We have free time and entertainment times. We even have an occasional party where we all dress up and stay up late into the night.

Not a day passes that I do not think of Lane. Many days I think I spot him somewhere out of the corner of my eye. A shadow around a corner. A cool breeze across my lips. My belly bulges now. When she moves you can watch her bump and roll inside. Liam is the most intrigued by the whole idea of a niece. He and Lizzie have finally become official. Surprisingly, Luke has warmed up to Sara. They train together most mornings. Carl has been allowed to train with us, with limitations. None of us trust him fully. We have at least found peace in walking the halls and sharing space with him.

Beth nearly runs the house without help from Kate. She is usually chasing down Beth to have something to do. A small place inside me will miss this. A family has developed where there were strangers and enemies. Most of it a is only façade though. I doubt things would have worked out this way had we all been allowed to go our separates ways all those months ago.

We are still unsure how it will work out to get Moloch to the willow tree. We have worked through hundreds of scenarios. Of course, they are always successful. Reality may not prove to work like it does in practice. My personal training hours have recently been shortened. I was able to keep up with the others without trouble until a strange pain in my side about a week ago. We now have an obstetrician who visits weekly or when called.

Somehow, Beth was able to convert one of the bedrooms into my very own labor and delivery room. This dilemma came as a shock to all of us. Though one of us should have realized it sooner. I cannot leave to a hospital. None of us can leave the grounds at all. We can make it to the end of the drive before an invisible barrier reminds us that we are prisoners. The staff members can come and go as they please. They would not even know if we had not filled them in. We rely on them for all our off-ground needs.

I have become close with a few of them. The older, more experienced, women always have advice for delivery and new mom tips. Tips I do not think I will be here to experience, but I appreciate the information. They enjoy telling me about their own children and grandchildren.

Now that my pregnancy has affected my ability to train, I stroll, leisurely around the grounds following the stone wall fence during the morning exercise routines of the others. My ability to feel their feelings has homed in so tightly that I can know who is feeling what at nearly all times.

I spend a lot of my time at the willow. Every day I speak the names of the ones we lost. Every morning I call out to Felicia. Hoping to see her again or receive some kind of sign. I am met with only silence.

I make my way from under the willow branches. A strange energy floats in the air. Something new has crossed the barrier. I pick up my pace to get inside. From outside the back entrance nothing seems awry. With my attention on high alert, I enter the main hall. The front entrance opens. Two people enter.

A shiver passes over my skin. The temperature in the room drops. I cross the space as the door behind them closes. The lighting adjusts. Moloch and Lane stand side by side. Something is wrong. Lane is different. Much like the last time I seen him, he stands still as a statue. The features on his face frozen in place. Not figuratively. The tattoos on his face are covered in a thin layer of ice. The lights in the hall sparkle and dance across the ice fractures like the sun against a morning frost.

His eyes too have changed. The light ice blue is now midnight. A deep darkness. Empty. He does not smile or rush to hold me like I had imagined he would on so many sleepless nights. I failed him. I should have gone to save him. I call out a warning to Liam in my mind.

The tattoo on my face freezes. No one else comes into the main hall. The staff are quiet and hidden. I can feel the emotions of my friends. There is an energy running through all of them. They know they are here but are waiting before they approach. We discussed this a few times. Do not make a stand of power against him. Well, now them. I reach out with my mind to cover them with protection.

We have practiced this a lot. It seems that if the powers used against it are physically harming, it only dampens the blow. The experience of my past attempts and our practice seems to be it is more of a mental protection. Without being able to test it fully we can only hope that, at the very least, our circle will be protected from mental attacks.

Moloch breaks the silence that has thickened in the large hall. "You have done well, my queen." He looks me up and down. His voice echoes against the walls. "It is amazing what the human body can do. Look at you." He looks at my stomach adoringly.

I want to vomit. "We weren't expecting you until the baby came." I push away the nausea. It is too early for them to be back.

"She will come soon. Lane wouldn't miss the birth of his child." He says as he begins to stroll the hallway. Admiring portraits and vases that line the walls and small tables. "This is all new?" He asks.

"We have a new designer on the team." I answer him. "I could give you a tour of all the modern design elements we have added." I keep my eyes on Lane. Waiting for him to do something. Anything.

"No, thank you." He says to me politely. "Has your design team created a room to deliver the child?" He asks me.

"Yes." I answer.

He nods toward Lane. Lane turns on his heel opens the door and nods outside. He returns to his spot and becomes motionless again. People begin to file in. Supay, Pacha, Brock, Kyle, Vira, and three others I do not recognize.

"We are starved from the trip. Will you have your staff whip us up something?" Moloch asks politely. The line of people passes me to the dining room.

Lane is the last one to pass me. He does not look my way. I try to feel his emotions. Sense anything of the man I love. Nothing. He is an impenetrable wall of power. A power that is not his. Moloch has done something to him. Changed him. He passes within inches of me. I hold back the urge to reach out and touch him.

They are here much earlier than I expected. I rush to the kitchen to inform the staff there. They start working in silence. Tension builds.

Thirty Two

Two days have passed since their arrival. They move around as if they are welcomed guests. I have seen little of Lane. When I do, he is always near Moloch's side. Liam is not able to reach him. He describes it as a wall. He can feel him on the other side, but he cannot find a way in.

Beth's first action was to call the obstetrician. She will now stay in the manor with the rest of us. We do not discuss it now that we have company, she understands that her only concern is to save the child. No matter what is happening or what condition I may be in. Dave and Luke were appointed as bodyguards during the early months of planning. Their jobs, if things look grim, is to protect my body at all cost.

Our circle has been on high alert the last forty-eight hours. We will not be able to keep this up much longer. The stress alone threatens to weaken us. We cannot wait for the child to be born. We must act now. We must return Moloch while all of us are strong enough to do so.

My body is healthy, and the baby is healthy. As we get closer to delivery time the doctor says the chances of decline in both of our health's will increase. She does not approve of me putting myself in danger but if there is a suitable time to risk it, it is now. Lizzie has also been added to the group of people that are to protect and save the child. Her healing abilities will be a necessity.

Extraordinarily little of this information has been passed verbally. Most of these measures have been in place since our first week of imprisonment. From here we all have to trust that we remember the things we practiced and follow the plan as close as we can.

I make my way through the manor. Stopping at each one of my allies. I find Liam. Through our mental connection I tell him I am going to the willow. *The time is here.* My tattoo tingles in his response. I find the rest with pointed looks and soft touches on their arms. They respond with nods, gentle smiles, and Lizzie wraps her arms around my neck.

In the main hall Lane is standing outside the entrance to the convention hall. I watch him as I pass. His presence intimidates me. He does not speak to me. He eyes do not follow my movements. I want to walk up to him. Scream in his face. Shake him by the shoulders. I want to save him. I want to push all caution aside and do what needs to happen to bring him back. *One life is not more important than the many.* I remind myself. Returning Moloch will hopefully release whatever hold he has on Lane.

I continue to the tree. I am going to it in one final attempt for guidance. For an easy answer to all our problems. One has not come before. I do not expect one now. A memory or a dream has kept me coming to this tree looking for answers. A thought that skirts away from when I reach out for it. I fear that what awaits my return is Aymara is not something we have planned for. None of us know how to plan for that side. My one short visit did not give me any answers to what happens after the tree.

    I kneel at the twisted trunk of the willow. I close my eyes. A prayer like pose. Minutes pass without change. I beg for Felicia to help me. *Tell me what to do next.* Silence. I let out a huff of disappointment. I open my eyes.

    The world around me is dark. The willow is gone. I am not alone. A deep darkness that seems to continue forever. I whip my head around wildly. A small source of light finally catches my attention. It gently sways in the distance. It begins to grow. Not grow, move closer. As it moves closer, she materializes. The light spreading to give form to her features. Her face begins to have definition. *Felicia.*

    "Child you have been difficult to get ahold of. I kept calling. You never answer." I am confused as she keeps talking. "He was able to leave a piece of his spirit here. In the shadows. He is stuck. We can't help him from this side." She pauses, the light that is her dims and then grows brighter again. "Guide him. Complete him. It could be the straw that breaks the camel's back." She fades away just as slowly as she came to form.

    I move my mouth to speak. I reach my arms out to her. My arms do not lift, my voice does not make a sound. I am not in the spirit realm. It is only a message from her. My mind scrambles to remember her words. To make sense of the nonsense. *It must be Lane. His spirit must be the one that is broken. The camel must be Moloch.* I need to get to him.

My eyes open. Liam is sitting right in front of me. "Don't scare me like that." He scolds. I flinch back from him.

"Felicia." I sputter. "Lane. We have to find Lane." My words become urgent.

"Hold on. Hold on. First are you ok?" I look at him and then myself. "You have been sitting here for hours. We have been taking turns sitting with you. We even had the doc come check your vitals."

I did not realize I had been gone so long. It all happened so quickly to me. A few minutes.

"I am fine." I stand. "Lane was able to leave a part of his spirit here. It broke him somehow. I knew he was here, and I ignored it." I scold myself for not realizing sooner. *How was I supposed to know?* "Moloch has taken over the rest of it. If we can find that part of Lane and put it back. He can find his way back to us. This could even be the key thing we need to catch Moloch off guard and finish this." I am nearly jogging back to the manor. "I knew I felt him here. I knew it."

Liam jogs to keep up with me. "Slow down, Jane. After all this time I think he would have found a way to us. How would he even know how to leave part of his spirit here?" Liam attempts to rationalize the situation.

"I don't think he knew what he was doing. It may not have even been on purpose. His spirit is lost in the shadows. That part of him probably doesn't have the ability to conceive the passing of time." Hope washes through me. Something I did not realize I had lost. I run straight through the main hall and upstairs to find Lizzie. "He could have been trying to reach us all along." I call down the stairs behind me.

I fill her in on what I have learned. It all comes out so quickly I have to repeat a lot of myself as she tries to understand. *Frustration.* We search late into the night. None of us are even sure what we are looking for. Lizzie's abilities to grow and heal have been the biggest help. She can sense his spirit.

We know that he is close. We just cannot pin him down. "For all we know he could be looking for us. His spirit does not have the limits of walls and obstacles. Every time we think we are close he could swoosh off to another area." Lizzie tries to explain.

Resting in the entertainment room, we all try to come up with any ideas on how to catch him. Liam comes up with the best idea yet, "The baby." He jumps from his seat in excitement. "He wouldn't have left the baby unprotected."

"If he was close to the baby, we would have found him by now." I say pointing at my stomach.

Lizzie looks thoughtful, "No, I don't think so. You said that you feel his presence. Is there a particular place that you feel him strongest?"

"His room." We all make our way there. We have already looked here. I sit on the bed and we all wait for anything to happen. The cool breeze that I sometimes feel does not happen. For a room filled with people, it is silent and still.

Liam starts pacing through the dressing room. Lizzie asks, "Where was the last place you talked to Lane before he went with Moloch?"

"In this room." I answer.

"No." Liam says as he comes to a stop in front of the sofa in the changing room. "Here, he was upset that you weren't concerned about the baby. At this point we didn't know if it was true yet."

I remember that I never had a chance to tell him about the pregnancy. We never got to talk about it. Does he even know about it now? Does he know he will have a daughter?

Liam continues. "He also opened up about the dreams. I do not get enough details to know the exacts, but he had been having them for some time. He finally decided to warn you. He sat here long after he sent you away." He examines the sofa for a long time.

These memories, I do not enjoy reliving. This was our last time together. Lane and I; we were arguing and upset. He sent me away to think. He sent me away knowing he was walking right into Moloch's plan. He sent me away because he knew he was going to sacrifice himself. For his daughter. He did not need a test to know that she was coming. He believed it from the moment there was mention of it.

I make my way to the sofa. I kneel in front of it. Trying to mimic the position I was in just before he asked for space. I close my eyes and focus. The darkness fills everything around me again. It happens so easily. Another light is in the distance. This time the light shines bright but does not move. I try to move toward it. I push my legs to move. Nothing happens. I feel like I am on a treadmill. Running full speed and getting nowhere. I call out to the light. I beg him to come to me. *Panic is not going to help.* I tell myself.

I close my eyes. I think about pulling him toward me. The feeling of taking Sara's power. I lock onto that thought. I pull against the energy flowing from the light and mentally hoist an invisible rope towards myself. I open my eyes to the ripple of energy between myself and his light. He slowly materializes, like Felicia did. Only much slower. If time is passing on the outside world, like it did before with her, I need to make this quick. His face finally has definition.

The tattoos are not on his skin. I hesitate for only a moment. He looks so much like Moloch without the tattoos. It makes sense that the tattoos would not be on his spiritual form. They are only physical. His eyes, though, they are the right color. His presence makes me feel love and hope. *Lane.* I can feel him. He does not feel the hope and love that I do. His eyes are full of confusion and fear. I must get him out of here now.

My voice does not work here. I push with my mind. Thinking, *hold on to this energy. Do not let go.* His eyes change. It is like he is only just now seeing me. I push harder, *Hold on tight. I will not let you go.* He looks at the space between us. He can see the energy too. His translucent hands hold on to the ripple of the invisible energy. He nods once. *I have to go back now. I have to take you back to your body. Please, do not let go.* I beg.

Thirty Three

I open my eyes. The empty sofa is sitting in front of me. My friends standing in a circle around me. Impatience ripples through the air. Luke starts talking. "We have to go. Moloch is angry. He is waiting for us in the convention hall."

"We have been trying to cover for you. He is threatening to drag you down there himself." Liam continues.

"How long was I gone?" I ask.

Lizzie answers. "A full day this time. We didn't think you would make it back."

I wish I could understand why the shadows and spiritual realm causes me to lose time but in Aymara, it took only seconds to complete a task.

"Did you find him?" Sara asks. An urgency in her tone.

"Yes, I have him." I answer. "I need to get to Lane."

"They are all in the hall. Every one of them." Luke says pointedly. "You won't be able to get to him in there."

"I have to." I answer. "I don't know how long he will hold on." I take a deep breath and stand with them.

I look at each one of them. Sara, Lizzie, Beth, Miley, Dave, Luke, and Liam. "Now, is the time." I look at each of them again. "I have to go now." I can feel the energy of Lane around me. I imagine holding on to it with all my strength.

"Then we all go now." Dave says strongly.

I am thankful for Dave. He is one of the strong ones. He will make sure the rest let me go. Liam is the one who understands exactly what I must do, but Dave will make sure it happens without sentiment getting in the way. I start to leave the room first.

"No." Liam says. *Spoke too soon.* I scold myself. "You enter that room last." *Whew, thank you Liam.*

We fall into order as we make our way to the convention hall. I feel the emotions of them shift. They push aside all worry and fear and each place determination in the front of their minds. We are ready.

∞∞∞

We pause outside of the doors to the convention hall. I look the group over once. I focus all my strength on protecting their minds. This time I see it. A blanket of energy drapes over them falling around their shapes. I do not know if this will protect them enough.

Collectively we let out a breath. Luke and Dave lead the way through the doors. Followed by Miley and Lizzie. Then Sara and Beth. With Liam by my side, we walk in last. Kate and Carl cross my mind briefly. I have not seen them since Moloch arrived. The time to worry about them has passed. *Focus.* I scold myself.

Moloch's people react quickly. They know we are not here to talk. The room seems larger somehow. None of us have entered here since Moloch took Lane away all those months ago. The chairs have been moved out completely. The thrones are all pushed back as far as the room will allow. Not one person is seated. Every person stands in a defensive pose. I wonder for a moment how long they have been standing here waiting on us.

Moloch stands center with Lane's soulless body at his right side. Everybody in his line of defense has a ripple of power growing around them. The ripples grow stronger. The waves grow higher picking up speed as they push toward my group. The waves interrupt each other, as they cross into one another's paths. Vira's ripple makes it to Dave and Luke. It hits my protective blanket and ripples away losing momentum. I focus on that blanket stronger.

"We are here for Lane." Dave announces.

"Ha!" Moloch mocks. "You think you can walk in here and make demands. Seems I should have come sooner. You all have gained a confidence not suiting to your competition." He lifts one arm in the air and snaps his fingers.

The room breaks out in a large rumbling of sounds. Dave's body shifts to stone. Luke puts his hands out in front of him. Miley shifts to her wolf form. Right in front of everyone. Her shirt and slacks rip away from her human body as the wolf's body bursts through the threads. She shakes her dense fir and snarls. The change is much quicker than I had imagined, she did not seem to experience pain. I shake away my awe and I force myself to focus.

Beth and Lizzie hold their arms out to their side's, palms facing the floor. Sara ducks down on the haunches of her feet. Liam does the same. This is the one part of our training that we had figured out. From here it would be all response to the situation. Liam and Sara, not having powers useful in a fight, we decided would protect themselves from attack. Try to cause diversions or warn of incoming danger. *The eyes in the back of our heads.* The setup is perfect. Now to do my part.

Starting first with Vira. *Take his power.* Remove the threat of mind control. The one thing that could turn us against each other. Then take every power that I can possibly grasp. Knowing the plan, the others do what they can to divert attention away and block me from attack. I reach out to Vira's mind. I quickly grasp the ripples of his energy. I catch him in a moment of internal panic as he realizes he cannot penetrate their minds. The process is slow. A few times I think I may lose my hold on him, as bodies move all around me. Crossing my path of vision. Vira yells out and falls to the floor in defeat as I consume the last of his power.

"There! There!" Sara yells at me over the commotion. I look where she is pointing. One of the new members of Moloch's group has his eyes targeted on me. Energy ripples around his body. I have to duck away as Luke sprays water at Kyle. Whose body is covered in his blue flame. Trying to advance on our huddle. I find the new man again and reach for his power with my mind.

He is stronger than Vira was. He fights against me. I feel him grabbing at my powers. Trying to pull mine from me. This is unexpected. I struggle against his power. I drop my mental hold on his energy and work on protecting mine. Miley senses my struggle or maybe Lizzie told her. Her large wolf body stretches and scrunches with her wide leaps. She tackles him to the ground, and I lose sight of them both.

I quickly scan the scene around me. Powers ripple the air. Bodies slam into each other. Yelling and grunts. Punches and kicks. *We should have taken this outside.* This room feels smaller than ever, even with the chairs removed. A shadow creeps through the people. Sniffing up the legs of my people. Supay moves through the crowd.

"Luke!" I yell. We do not know enough about Supay other than do not let him touch anyone.

Luke reacts, spraying Supay with water. It works for the time. The shadow rushes back to Supay. I see an opening to Lane. I risk dashing towards him. He stands unmoving. He has not reacted to any of the events happening around him. His body does not have the rippling energy around it. Too soon, I feel relief that I am almost to him.

His arm comes out from his body as I close the small distance left between us. His open hand wraps around my neck. The momentum of my body causes my lower half to swing forward against the sudden stop of my upper half. He lifts me easily into the air. My airways close. Pressure builds in my skull. Stars float in my peripheral vision. I search his eyes for anything remaining of my Lane. Only an endless sea of midnight blue. I struggle to focus on putting Lane back as my mind grows hazy.

    I reach one hand out toward him. Stretching to touch his forehead. *Please still be there.* I think to myself. A shadow begins to fill my eyes. I am about to lose consciousness. I reach inside for any strength still left. My fingertip barely brushes his forehead. His head snaps back farther away from me. *That was my only chance.* The failure falls in my heart and darkness fills my vision.

Thirty Four

My eyes flutter open. My throat and chest burn in pain. The world around me bounces wildly. A new pain registers in my legs. I am being dragged across the ground. Stones and sticks pulling at the skin being exposed through ripped fabric. I crane my neck to look up. Kyle is dragging me by the back of my shirt. I am like a rag doll dangling from his hand. Ahead of us Moloch leads the way. We are in the farthest part of the property heading for the gate that will lead us to the tunnels.

He is taking me away from the willow. I panic and then control my emotions to consider my next move. If he were able to trap me inside the grounds, he could also trap me outside the grounds. *I cannot let that happen.* I focus on Kyle's power. This one is easy. Possibly because I have already taken some. His powers come to me without fight. He crumples to the ground with a shout. Dropping me hard on my face. I struggle to make my sore legs work under me.

I only make it a few steps back before Moloch yells, "You are making all of this a lot harder on yourself." He starts to make his way toward me. Backing away, I nearly trip over something on the ground. A stone or tree root. "Your friends will all be dead soon. I only need the child." He bellows.

He is lying. I tell myself. If that were true, he would not be running away with only me and Kyle. Kyle writhes in pain on the ground. For the first time I notice his clothes are dripping wet. Moloch was losing back there. *Back there. I have to get back.* My friends are still in danger. I shake my head to clear it. Moloch thinks I am shaking my head in disbelief. *I must return Moloch first.*

I turn to run back. I can feel him running behind me. Closing the distance quickly. My stomach aches at the exertion. I push aside the worry about the child. For now, I can only hope that she makes it through the other side of this. I push aside the truth that I have known for a long time. I will not be here to make sure she is safe. I will not be here to raise her. Right now, I need my focus on getting Moloch away from here. I can only hope that the ending part of our planning works out. That Lizzie can make a way to the tree. I build my fire inside me. Pulling it into a ball in my hands.

Moloch is tight on my heels. I turn and release the ball of fire at him. He stumbles as it hits him in the chest. I break through the tree line of the woods. The willow standing tall, ten yards or so ahead of me, gently waving her long branches. Moloch growls behind me and pushes harder to close the distance between us. Not as close to the tree as I had hoped, Moloch's fingers hook in the neck of my shirt. Jerking me down to the ground backwards. The wind is knocked out of me with the impact. My lungs violently expand trying to pull air back into them.

Arms come around me. I roll into him to throw his balance off. He falls and latches on to me. My back to him he lurches me off the ground. I kick my legs wildly. He pins my arms under his. He turns putting our backs to the willow, with intentions to go back into the woods. I plant my feet hard into the ground and push with all my might. Knocking both of us backwards. He loses his balance. My head slams hard against his chin, as we hit the ground. His hold on me loosens. I cannot help the moment of excitement that I feel when I look around. We are under the willow.

The impact of my head against his chin must have made him see stars. He is holding both hands to his head and he seems like he is lost. I take advantage of his position. I grab the closest part of his body to me. His ankle. I pull his weight across the ground. My entire mid-section screams out in pain. A tightening in the muscle's cripples me for a second. His mind is clearing. I am running out of time. I let the force of gravity help as I grip his ankle tighter and fall towards the trunk.

I take a deep breath, pushing aside the pain in my midsection, ignoring the pain in my head. As quickly as I can manage, I free one hand from the grip around his ankle and stretch my arm toward the trunk of the tree. He resists and my belly contracts again. His free leg swings hard into my chest. Knocking the breath out of me. I fight against my body's reaction to curl up.

A strange guttural grunt comes from my throat as I push against the ground with both feet and attempt one last hurl of strength. My fingers touch the trunk.

A flash of light sends us both flying, breathless, away from the tree. We both land in exhausted heaps in a garden. A voice booms in the air all around my head. I reach first for my midsection. The bulge of the child is gone. My stomach flat under my shirt. The voice booms again. I look for its source this time. A giant of a man stands over both of us.

"Chaska! What have you done?" His voice booms.

In his shadow, my memories flood through my mind. The separation from my human form allowing it all. Shocking at first. My mind is slow to remember how to process it all. He is my father, Pachacutec. We live here in Aymara. Amongst many other gods. Many of our legends tell of our kind visiting other worlds. In search of power. Convincing the beings on them to worship us. Similar to many of the stories back on earth about magical beings and gods bringing wealth and power to their lands. Here though, those that go on these expeditions are looked down on by our kind. It is shameful to parade yourself, to sell yourself, to such a life. You could gain power on that earth, but you are forever banished from places of power here in Aymara. If caught, you are placed in a prison of isolation. Exiled from ever returning.

My father had announced my marriage to someone I did not want to marry. This upset Moloch, who thought he could convince my father to choose him to be my betrothed. Moloch was once a friend of mine. *My most trusted friend*, I realize. I did not feel the same way about him. My rejection and my father not choosing him caused him to lash out in anger. He ran to the other realm knowing I would follow him. He thought we would find a way to each other there. He manipulated his power. Took advantage of exiled gods of our kind. Somehow, he freed them. All to finally have me as his wife.

My father is not aware of the events that took me across the realms. He does not usually leave his position.

Here in Aymara time moves differently. Our minds do not require constant entertainment. We do not need companionship to feel complete. Most of the Aymaran people live in small groups and still prefer solitude within those groups. I remember my place. Father stays in his quarters, which is more like a workshop. My sister enjoys the water. I can always find her by the river's edges. My place is here. In this garden. It looks different now. The intrusion of my father and Moloch stains the memories of this sacred, to me, place. But this is the Aymaran in me. My human self. The one I left behind, would not care about this place at all. She loves only Lane. *I love Lane.*

The look on my father's face brings me back to the issue at hand. He only comes out to send those into solitude who deserve it. There is never a hearing. A decision about my destiny has already been made. What I did is unforgivable. I will be banished with Moloch. Moloch will win. Suddenly, my body begins to violently convulse. Two forms pull away from my body with a formidable force. I do not feel pain. Only a discomfort. Two men materialize from the forms.

My father's face turns even more menacing. He confuses what has just happened as my fault. As if I carried these two with me across the realms. I start to explain. My father faces Moloch and the two other men now standing among us.

His voice booms, "Exile." Six large men materialize, one on either side of the three of them. The guards of our realm.

Strong warriors. They lead the three men away. Moloch looks over his shoulder at me and grins. He knows what he has done. He knows what my father will do. My father turns his attention back to me. If I allow him to speak, I know the words of the short speech that will come. I will be exiled for crossing realms.

My father will not go into more details than that. This me, my Aymaran self, loves him deeply. The eyes that look back at me are not the ones I am familiar with being pointed in my direction. I have brought shame to myself and him. I will quickly be forgotten here. Never allowed to return to my garden.

I am not done back on earth. He will not listen. Even if I could get a word in, he would only say that the damage caused would heal itself. Which could be true. I cannot allow him to say the words that are building in his chest. I will not be able to fight against the warriors here. My powers are nothing against their strength. His chest fills with air ready to announce my fate. I jump to my feet and dive back the few feet to the willow tree of this garden.

Thirty Five

My fingers brush its rough trunk, and I am back under the willow at the manor. The tree seems different. The branches sway gently in the wind. A glow surrounds everything I see. A body lays crumpled at my feet. An arm stretched awkwardly out from it. Her face is down. Her legs curled under her. Her other arm wrapped around her midsection. She does not move. She is not breathing. She is me. The body too broken for me to return.

I hear someone moving fast. Feet pounding the ground as he pushes the branches aside and falls to the ground next to my body. "Liam."

His head snaps up to find me. "Jane?" He looks back down at my crumpled body.

"She needs Lizzie and the doctor." I tell him. "Now." I add when he does not move right away. He scurries out. I sit with my lifeless body.

I place my hand on my stomach. No longer mine. This body now only has one thing left to do. Protect the baby. Under my hand, I feel small thumps. The baby is weak, but alive. Minutes pass before Liam bursts back through the branches of the willow. Lizzie behind him.

Lizzie drops to her knees beside my body. She quickly assesses the situation. Urgency pitches the tone in her voice. "I can't save her. Help me carry her to the delivery room." She yells at him.

Liam looks at my body and then at me. The connection we had, gone. He bends to lift my body carefully. With tears in his eyes, he turns and carries my body away. Lizzie stays tight on his heels.

On the other side of the branches, the air is disrupted by an earth shattering, gut wrenching, human howl turned to sob. I try to reach out, to feel for his emotions. That connection is gone too. I know it is Lane. I can feel the heartbreak. Anyone who may be near can feel the heartbreak that pulses through the air.

Dave passes through the branches of the willow. Miley follows behind him, returned to her human form. I want to tell her how amazing her power is. How beautiful it is to watch a human become a powerful being. The looks on their faces stops me. I do not know what they expected to find here, but it was not me. Not like this. Dave, the one who is always ready to do the challenging thing, steps directly in front of me. His clothes are dirty and torn. His breathing is heavy. The fight that I left must have recently ended.

Dave breaks the silence. "Is it done?" I nod. "He needs you." He thumbs toward where Lane is standing on the other side of the willow branches. "We know what you have to do now."

Miley's eyes drop to the ground. "I am proud to have been able to be here for all of you."

The exhaustion is easy to see in their stances. "It is all over now. This will not hurt if you do not resist." I cautiously hold my hands out, palms toward both. I carefully link to the energies around them. Dave's power does not come to me as the powers of the others did. I watch curiously as his energy returns to the earth below his feet. Miley's also does not come to me. Instead, the glowing silhouette of a wolf stretches away from her. The body shakes before trotting off through the branches. I watch in awe at the still branches of the willow. The wolf's body, a spirit, does not disturb the living branches. This must explain why only two forms came out of me in Aymara. The woman that ran from me during my first visit. She must have been the Aymaran form of Sara's power. Kyle's power must have been returned to the earth's spiritual realm.

Dave wraps his arm around Miley's shoulder. Her head still down. "Thank you." I say to them as they push the branches aside to pass under them. They do not look back.

I pass through the branches of the willow. Like the wolf, the branches do not move, I walk through them as if they are not even there. The world looks different now. Everything living seems to have a glow around it. The grass, the trees, even a butterfly flutters by surrounded by a bright purple haze. The nonliving or man-made things are grey in color. No glow, not even a reflection of light bouncing off them. A dull nothing.

A sob draws my attention to the ground in front of me. Lane is on his knees facing the manor. His fists balled tight against the ground below him. The glow around him pulses. His power mixed with his emotions of anguish.

"She will need you." I say to him.

He jumps to his feet and spins around to look at me. "Jane?" Shock, fear, and then calm pass across his features.

I see this. Different from before. This time it is because I recognize the changes in his features. Not because of a power that links me to his emotions. I move close to him. Face to face we look at one another a long time. Unsure if I can feel him in this form. I gently touch my fingertips to his chin.

"She needs you." I repeat with the coolness of his cheek under my touch.

His eyes are the blue they were meant to be. His tattoos the dark color of Liam's ink. The layer of ice, that was there when I last seen him, is gone.

"It was stupid of me to do it. I should not have left you. I thought it would be for the best. I did not understand what it meant until it was too late. When you put me back together, you were already gone." He pauses. "You are dead." He puts this together in his mind. I do not have to tell him what has happened. He knows.

"I am not dead. The body that carries your child is dead. That is not me. It never really was. Nothing of the past matters now." I look at him and take his face in both of my hands. "I cannot stay. I have to finish this."

"I can't do this without you." He whispers.

"She can't do this without you." I gesture to the manor where my lifeless body is being prepared to deliver new life to this world. "She will be your connection with me. I will always be with you. The bond with the people around you will remain strong. They love the child like you do. She will hold you all together." I tell him.

He wraps his arms around me. It feels so right to be in his arms. He leans down to kiss me. I kiss him back. Knowing this will be the last time I can kiss him. I pull back slightly.

"I have to take it now."

He kisses me deeper one last time. His energy is harder to grasp. His emotions making them thrash from my hold. One by one I watch as his tattoos glow bright. Each with its own line of energy leading into me. The tattoos are from my world. Gods there once used them to enhance their own powers. It is now forbidden along with realm travel. I remember my father telling me the stories. When they have all returned to me, the only mark still present is the one on the inside of his wrist. The scar that was below the first tattoo.

"Go to her." I whisper.

Thirty Six

The world around me shifts. My desire to meet my daughter pulls me through space and time. I am standing in a nursery. The dressing room of Lane's bedroom. It has been converted into a nursery. The obstetrician carries a wrapped bundle over to the basinet. Liam is sitting patiently in the bedroom. Waiting for the doctor to leave. She says something to Liam on her way out. He nods.

"I know you are here." He says after the door closes.

"I came to see her. I am glad you are here too." I say to him.

"He made it to see her birth." He tells me. "I promised to stay with her until he is fed and clean. I don't think he would have ever left her side." He almost sounds like he is talking to himself. "Are you ready to take it? It doesn't work anymore anyway." He finishes in a huff.

"Yes." I answer him.

"Do you know that once it's done, we can't see you anymore? Dave, Miley, and Lane all say so." He looks concerned.

"I didn't know." I answer him. I push aside the sadness that I feel. *I should have spent more time with Lane.* "I would like to see her." I change the subject.

He nods. I approach the small bed cautiously. This new knowledge has changed how I thought I would approach the rest of all of them. This is what must be done. I look down into the bassinet. Her amber eyes are open wide. Her cheeks are full and pink. *She is perfect.* I reach my fingertips down to feel the soft skin of her head. Only a small amount of yellow hair protects her head.

"She looks like her mother." Liam says from behind me. The baby coos lightly. Her eyes looking all around, looking for anything to focus on. I lean in closer to her. She spots me. As I watch, her eyes begin to register whatever her mind is capable of perceiving as recognition, a tiny ripple of energy ripples around her.

I step back with a jerk. Am I strong enough to take this energy from this little creature? It is a part of me that is in her. Maybe even some of Moloch. It is dangerous to leave it here. It is irresponsible of me not to take it.

I turn to Liam. I place one hand on his shoulder. "Thank you, Liam." I say to him. Saying it before I take his energy. Now that I know they cannot see me when it is done.

"It isn't for you anymore, it's for her." He answers. I know he will be there for her.

I pull his energy into me. His will be one I have to return to Aymara along with Lane's. Thinking about returning there scares me. I look down at the beautiful child in the tiny bed. I do not take her energy. *I will come back for hers.* I lie to myself.

I make my way through the manor, taking the

energies that are to be returned to Aymara. Setting the energies free that are of this world. The battle that took place during my personal battle with Moloch, was successful. Luke fills me in on the details. He shows me to the convention hall where they have held some prisoners. Supay, Pacha and Brock escaped. I assure him that I will find them all, in time. They are now my responsibility. Of the ones that have been captured, Carl is watching over. I do not introduce myself or explain what I am about to do. I finish this group quickly.

I find Lizzie in the clearing. Staring longingly at the willow. "Glad I found you." I say, to gently announce myself.

"I heard you were making the rounds." She says to me without looking at me. "He is waiting for you." She points at the willow. "I think he will always be waiting for you."

I walk in front of her to face her. Tears stream down her cheeks. "He won't always. She will now fill my void." I take a deep breath. "Lizzie, when I return to Aymara, I will be exiled for my crimes. I will never be able to return. He will need all of you."

"Of course. Liam would never leave him and especially not her." She assures me. Then asks, "Do you have to go back?"

I hug her to me. She hugs me back. I wish I could stay. I wish I could just hop back in my body and live this life with them. I pull her energy to me. It seeps away from us into the ground. My arms that once squeezed her, squeeze around myself. Her eyes look through me instead of at me. I did not watch any of the others faces like this. I turn away. The pain is more than I can bear.

    Under the branches of the willow, I find Lane. He is standing with his arms across his chest. "Lane." I say his name aloud.

    "I know you are there. I cannot hear you. I feel your warmth." His response hurts a place deep inside me. A shadow of the person I was when I was with him. A person I can never be again. Her heart is breaking. Somehow in this form it feels separate from me. Inside me but not attached. He breathes deeply. "She is beautiful. Perfect in every way. I will not let her down like I did you. I won't fail her." He promises.

    I close the distance between us. I place my hand on his cheek. It passes through him. I settle for placing my lips close to his. Hoping that he can feel me here. "I love you." I say to him. Knowing he cannot hear me.

    "I will love you forever." It is not in response to me. Rather, an announcement he makes. He walks away.

    I wonder for a moment how it would feel to cry in this form? Is it something I can even do? From behind me, a voice calls to me. I turn to see Felica moving through air. She seems far away under the umbrella of the willow. She closes the distance slowly. "It is time to close this gateway. I will guide you to the others that need your help, and we will give you passage home."

    I hesitate. "I cannot return to Aymara." I confess.

    "You must return them. It is the only way." She scolds.

    "I will." I know what my future holds. I know that

once the job is complete, I have to return. I still do not want to.

"If you do not, your soul will be lost without a connection here. You will be that broken spirit in the cabin. The sentence that awaits you on Aymara, I fear there is nothing I can help you with when that path lies ahead of you." She is telling the truth. She is not angry or disappointed.

This is my reality. Once all the energies from Aymara have been returned, my own energy will only have two options: Get stuck between realms. Serve the exile my father will give me. Unable to see it through the branches of the willow I look longingly back toward the manor. Imagining the baby cooing softly in her warm bed.

Felicia takes my hand. Together we close the gateway.

Thirty Seven

Lane

Things would be different if it were not for me. I was stubborn and ignorant. If only I could have been a better man. If only I would have listened to her or my brother. If only.

That is my life now. Full of ifs. It continues though. That was the point of all this. Life to continue. At the cost of her life. One life for all of ours. There are so many things that went unsaid. Things that I will never be able to clear from my mind.

The manor stands empty. The grounds go unkept. I cannot bring myself to sell it. I cannot bring myself to burn it to the ground. I cannot bring myself to stroll the halls, or even cross the threshold of the wide front door. As far as I know, no one else can either.

The last time I stood within its borders was the day she left. I stood beside the willow as it started to change. The warmth of her fading from my lips. The branches swayed. Then they wound around itself. A darkness spread over the remains. The gateway to her closed. The finality of it all, too quick. I wanted to stop her. Beg for more time.

With a sigh, I moved on. The ones of us who fought with her through the end, followed suit. We made a home for ourselves in the small town that Lizzie was always talking about. Lizzie and Liam. Luke and Sara. Even Beth, Miley, and Dave decided to stay.

They used to tell me stories about that day. The last day. We do not know if she has finished her mission. All who we knew that had powers either do not anymore or have disappeared. Kate being one of the ones we have not seen. None of them can remember if they had seen her in the manor on that day at all.

Anyhow, it made sense for me to return to the house I owned here. It is big enough for what we need. It is close to the small town and not far from the manor. Great schools and a united community. Lizzie was right about the number of others who had powers living here. We have built a strong bond with most of them as we have learned to cope with normal lives.

We have healed. Liam and Lizzie even have a child of their own. Luke is no longer the hot head he once was. This town is making him soft, we tease him.

I think we all still look for her. A sign that she could return. Holding on to a hope that this reality without her is not the end. This hope stems from the only piece of her that remains.

Her. She has hair the color of amber. Eyes that shine gold in the light. Her smile lights up the night. Her cries break hearts for miles. Wilted flowers bloom in her presence.

My life was shattered and then saved on the day

she was born. She puts my pieces back together, every day. I will guard over her with my life. As will everyone who has ever had the graces of meeting her.

She will be four tomorrow. I like to think her mother will be nearby. I never see her. I feel her there. A shadow out of the corners of our eyes. A warm breeze across our cheeks. Of course, this is just something I tell myself. It is what I tell the little girl who calls me daddy. I tell her to look for her mother everywhere. On the wings of a butterfly, in the stars, and most of all in her heart.

In our back yard, we planted a willow. It stands four feet tall this year. Its trunk has started to twist. Its short, scarce, branches gently bend toward the ground. Here is where I think of her the most. Here is where I feel closest to her.

Under the willow is Hope's favorite place to play.

End

Hope Under The Willow

a novel

Book One

Acknowledgement

Thank you to every single person who has been by my side. Whether in person or virtually (that is a thing now), each one of you has helped to create the person I am today. The list is too long but to mention a few:

Christian, I know, I know, another venture I have dragged you by the arm with me as I have gone. You are the only person I ever want to pull along my side. I love you.

My children, the way you are always looking over my shoulders truly inspired many chapters in my book, currently it is inspiring your acknowledgement.

Wanda, Christina, Caitlin, Sarah... you do not even realize how much I have come to lean on the four of you. You are my crutches when my knees are weak.

Hey Ma! One day you will have to actually read these things. Or not, you know it is up to you. To all my other moms and all my dads of course this would not be a thing without all of you.

Finally, Kevin, thank you for relighting my creative bug that was getting burnt out on the work that was lain out in front of me. Your images brought color and life and inspiration back into my soul just when I needed it. I hope every person who lays eyes on them can feel the same impact that I feel every time I look at them.

Lastly thank me. Thank me for taking the plunge no matter how embarrassing it may have been in the start. Thank me for putting in the hard work and trusting in a wonderful team full of support and creativity. Thank me for not letting the worst year in history of years take me into the darkness and hold me there for all of eternity.

Thank you, Hope.

About The Author

Amanda J Kelley

Author of Hope's Trilogy. Amanda has discovered a freedom and release in writing.

Residing in the beautiful mountains of Northwest Georgia, she is raising her two children and dog Lola.

A passion for writing that was always pushed to the bottom of the list has now been released in a rare opportunity of free time and the isolations of quarantine. Her debut novel in January 2021, Hope Under the Willow, will be proceeded by two more novels to complete Hope's Trilogy.

And she does not plan to stop there.

Follow Amanda J Kelley
instagram- @amanda_j_kelley
facebook- @amandajkelleyauthor
twitter- @amandajkelley1

Books In This Series

Hope's Trilogy

The balance between realms is teetering. Is Jane the one that can restore it? Follow her on the journey across the realms as she attempts save the ones that she loves.

Hope Under The Willow; A Novel

She remembers nothing of her childhood. For the past fifteen years she has managed well enough. Or so she thought.

Her addiction to pills has kept her mind clouded from searching for the right answers. Now though, Jane must discover who she really is. With a clear mind and the love of her life by her side, will she find hope?

The balance between realms is teetering. The Elders seem to think the Fallen Angel will bring more power to Earth. Others think the Fallen is here to remove the other worldly powers that have found their way to Earth. Is she the one they are all searching for?

Hope In Between; Three Realms

Her father has kept his past a secret. When she discovers some strange paperwork, her best friend convinces her to search for answers.

Is she ready to face the truth? Her father's past is

full of skeletons and people with unique abilities. And her mother...

Hope Willow learns that her mother gave her own life to save the lives of everyone else. But was that sacrifice in vain? Are the powerful ones returning?

Hope Is Lost; Aymara

Chaska has finally returned to Aymara. She expects to be swiftly charged with the crime of crossing realms and sentenced to life in exile.

When that does not happen, she grows suspicious of the reasons. She journeys across the realm of Hanan for answers. Will she finally restore balance to the three realms?

Printed in Great Britain
by Amazon